Praise for Real Life

'A magnificent, resilient young heroine.'
Le Figaro

'A sense of rhythm, hard-hitting words,
and vitriolic humor.'
COLINE SERREAU, director of *Chaos*

'Always at the limit between the naïveté of a
child and the profundity of those of us who
have already seen too much.'
VÉRONIQUE CARDI, Publisher

'It's an impressive debut novel, poetic and violent
at the same time, with great visual force.'
GIOVANNA CANTON, Publisher

'I read the novel in one go. What a hypnotizing
voice!'
CRISTINA DE STEFANO, Literary Scout

'Bitter, raw, and fast-paced: a tale that's filled
with a hunger for life.'
ALAIN LORFÉVRE, *La Libre Belgique*

'When the innocence of fairy tales meets the
terror of a Stephen King thriller.'
BERNARD LEHUT, *RTL*

REAL LIFE

Adeline Dieudonné

REAL LIFE

Translated from the French
by Roland Glasser

WORLD EDITIONS
New York, London, Amsterdam

Published in the USA in 2020 by World Editions LLC, New York
Published in the UK in 2020 by World Editions Ltd., London

World Editions
New York/London/Amsterdam

Printed by Lake Book, USA

Library of Congress Cataloging in Publication Data is available

ISBN 978-1-64286-047-4

First published as *La vraie vie* in France in 2018 by L'Iconoclaste,
Paris.

Twitter: @WorldEdBooks
Facebook: WorldEditionsInternationalPublishing
Instagram: @WorldEdBooks
www.worldeditions.org

Book Club Discussion Guides are available on our website.

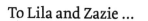

To Lila and Zazie ...

OUR HOUSE HAD four bedrooms. There was mine, my little brother Sam's room, that of my parents, and the one with the carcasses.

Deer calves, wild boar, stags. And antelope heads, of all sorts and sizes, including springboks, impalas, gnus, oryxes, and kobus. A few zebras minus their bodies. On a platform stood a complete lion, its fangs clamped around the neck of a small gazelle.

And in a corner was the hyena.

Stuffed she may have been, yet she was alive, I was sure of it, and she delighted in the terror she provoked in any gaze that met her own.

In the framed photographs on the wall, my father posed proudly with various dead animals, holding his rifle. He always took the same stance: one foot on the beast, fist on hip, the other hand victoriously brandishing the weapon. All of which made him appear more like a rebel fighter high on genocidal adrenaline than a father.

The centerpiece of his collection, his pride and joy, was an elephant tusk. I had heard him tell my mother one evening that the hardest part wasn't killing the elephant. No. Killing the beast was as easy as slaughtering a cow in a subway corridor. The real difficulty had been making contact with the poachers and avoiding the patrolling game wardens. And then removing the tusks from the still-warm body: utter carnage. It had all cost him a small fortune. I suppose that's why he was so proud of his trophy. Killing the elephant was so expensive he'd had to split the cost with another guy. They left with a tusk each.

I liked to stroke the ivory. It was silky smooth and large. But I had to do it behind my father's back. We were forbidden from entering the carcass room.

* * *

My father was huge with broad shoulders, the build of a slaughterman. He had a giant's hands. Hands that could have ripped the head off a chick the way you'd pop the cap on a Coke bottle. Besides hunting, my father had two passions in life: television and Scotch whisky. When he wasn't scouring the planet for animals to kill, he plugged the TV into speakers that had cost as much as a small car, a bottle of Glenfiddich in his hand. And the way he talked *at* my mother, you could have replaced her with a houseplant and he wouldn't have known the difference.

My mother lived in dread of my father.

I think that's pretty much all I can say about her, leaving aside her obsession with gardening and miniature goats. She was a thin woman, with long limp hair. I don't know if she existed before meeting him. I imagine she did. She must have resembled a primitive life form—single-celled, vaguely translucent. An amoeba. Just ectoplasm, endoplasm, a nucleus, and a digestive vacuole. Years of contact with my father had gradually filled this scrap of nothing with fear.

Their wedding photos always intrigued me. As far back as I can remember, I can see myself studying the album in search of a clue. Something that might have explained this weird union. Love, admiration, esteem, joy, a smile ... something. I never found it. In the pictures, my father posed as in his hunting photographs, but without the pride. An amoeba doesn't make a very impressive trophy, that's for sure. It isn't hard to catch one: a bit of stagnant water in a glass, and presto!

When my mother got married, she wasn't frightened yet. It seemed as though someone had just stuck her there, next to this guy, like a vase. As I grew older, I also wondered how this pair had conceived two children: my brother and me. Though I very soon stopped asking myself because the only image that came to mind was a late-night assault on the kitchen table, reeking of whisky. A few rapid, brutal, not exactly consenting jolts, and that was that.

In the main, my mother's function was to prepare the meals, which she did like an amoeba might, with neither creativity nor taste, but lots of mayonnaise. Ham and cheese melts, peaches stuffed with tuna, deviled eggs, and breaded fish with instant mashed potatoes. Mainly.

OUR GARDEN BACKED onto Little Gallows Wood and a small valley, all green and brown, its two slopes forming a large *V* with dead leaves piled up at the bottom. At the end of the valley, half-buried beneath the dead leaves, was Monica's house. Sam and I often went to see her. She once told us that the *V* had been formed by a dragon's claw, a very long time ago. The dragon had scraped out the valley after being driven mad with sorrow. Monica was good at telling stories. Her long gray hair danced across the flowers on her dress, and her bracelets jingled on her wrists.

"An awfully long time ago, not very far from here, on a mountain that is now gone, there lived a pair of gigantic dragons. These two dragons loved each other so much that at night they sang strange songs of intense beauty, as only dragons know how. But this scared the folk living down on the plain, and they could no longer sleep. One night, when the two lovers had dozed off after singing their hearts out, they came, those morons, tiptoeing along with their torches and pitchforks, and they killed the female. In his fury and grief, the male scorched the entire plain, killing everyone—men, women, and children. Then he ripped at the earth with his claws, scouring out these valleys. Since then, the vegetation has grown back, and people live here once more, but the claw marks remain."

The surrounding woods and fields were littered with scars of varying depth.

The story frightened Sam.

Some nights he would come snuggle in my bed because he thought he'd heard the dragon song. I explained that it was just a story, that dragons didn't really exist. That Monica had told it to us because she liked old tales, but that not everything was real. Yet deep down I had the shiver of a doubt. And I always dreaded that I would see my father return from one of his hunts with a female dragon head. But to reassure Sam, I played the older sister and whispered, "Stories exist to contain everything that frightens us. That way we can be sure those things won't happen in real life."

I liked going to sleep with his little head right under my nose so I could smell the scent of his hair. Sam was six years old, I was ten. Brothers and sisters are usually at each other's throats, riven by jealousy, fighting, whining, crying. Not us. I loved Sam with the devotion of a mother. I guided him, and told him everything I knew; that was my mission as his big sister. It was the purest form of love that could exist. A love that expects nothing in return. Indestructible.

He was always laughing, with his tiny baby teeth. And each time, his laughter warmed me like a mini power plant. So I made him puppets from old socks, invented funny stories, and put on little shows just for him. I tickled him too, to hear him laugh. Sam's laughter could heal any wound.

* * *

Monica's house was half-swallowed by ivy. A pretty sight. Sometimes the sunlight falling through the branches resembled fingers caressing it. I never saw the sun's fingers on my own house, or on the other houses in the neighborhood. We lived in a development called "The Demo." Fifty gray detached houses lined up like tombstones. My father called it "the Demucky."

Up until the 1960s, this was all wheat fields. In the early 1970s the development sprouted like a wart, in less than six months. It was a pilot project, at the cutting edge of prefabricated technology. The Demo. Demo of I don't know what. Those who had built it must have had something to prove at the time. Maybe it actually reflected their aims back then. But twenty years later all that remained was the muck. The beauty, if there ever was any, had dissolved, washed away by the rain. The street formed a big square, with inner houses and outer houses. And then all around lay Little Gallows Wood.

Our house was one of the outer houses, on a corner. It was a little better than the others because it was the one that the architect of the Demo had designed for himself.

But he didn't live there long. It was larger and lighter, too, with wide patio doors. And a cellar. Seems silly, said like that, but a cellar is an important thing. It prevents groundwater rising up through the walls and rotting them. The houses of the Demo smelled of old damp swimming towels forgotten in a sports bag. Our house didn't smell bad, but it did have the animal carcasses. I sometimes wondered if I wouldn't have preferred a house that stank.

Our garden was also bigger than the others. On the lawn was an inflatable swimming pool, which looked like a fat lady who had fallen asleep in the sun. Come winter, my father would empty it and pack it away, leaving a wide circle of brown grass. And at the bottom of the garden, just before the wood, there was the goat pen: a bank covered in creeping rosemary. It contained three young nanny goats: Cookie, Josie, and Nutmeg. But soon there'd be five because Nutmeg was in kid.

My mother had had a billy goat brought over to service Nutmeg, and this had caused no end of trouble with my father. Something odd occurred with my mother when it came to her goats: a kind of maternal instinct would gush from deep within her, making her capable of standing up to my father. Whenever that happened, he always looked like a teacher outdone by their student. Mouth open, he vainly sought a comeback. He knew that every passing second depleted his authority a little more, like a wrecking ball taken to a building blighted by dry rot. His open mouth would twist a little, producing a kind of growl that smelled like a skunk's burrow. At that moment, my mother would realize she had won. She would pay for it later, but for now that little victory was hers, although she didn't appear to derive any particular joy from it, and simply returned to her amoebal activities.

* * *

Nutmeg was in kid and Sam and I were overexcited by the imminent birth. We watched for the slightest sign announcing the new kids' arrival. He giggled as I explained how the little ones would be born:

"They will come out of her privates. It'll

look like she's pooping, but instead of poop, two baby goats will come out."

"But how did they get into her tummy?"

"They didn't, she made them with the billy goat. They were very much in love."

"But he was here for less than a day, they didn't even know each other, they couldn't have been in love."

"Oh yes they could. It's called love at first sight."

IF YOU CROSSED Little Gallows Wood then went through the field without being seen by the farmer, you got to the big slope of yellow sand. And if you went down it, hanging onto plant roots, you entered the labyrinth of broken cars. There, too, you had to make sure you weren't seen.

It was a vast metal boneyard, and I really liked the place. As I stroked the cars' shells, I would imagine them as a heap of creatures, motionless yet sentient. Sometimes I talked to them, especially the new ones. I told myself they must need reassuring. Sam would help me. The pair of us could spend whole afternoons talking to the cars. Some had been there a long time, so we got to know them well. There were those that were virtually unmarked, and others that were slightly damaged. And then there were those that were totally wrecked, hood ripped open, body shredded, as if chewed up by some huge dog.

My favorite was the green car devoid of both its roof and its seats. It looked as though it had been scraped clean at hood level, like foam on a glass of beer. I wondered what could have sliced it like that. Sam liked the "Boom-a-roller," as he called it. We would imagine that this funny old Boom-a-roller had been put into a giant washing machine, but without water. It was dented all over. Sam and I would get inside and pretend we were in the washing machine along with the car. I would take the wheel and cry "Boom-a-roller! Boom-a-roller! Boom-a-roller!" while bouncing up and down on the seat to make the car shake. And Sam's magic laughter would climb all the way to the top of the slope of yellow sand. At which point we knew we had to skedaddle because if the owner heard us, it wouldn't be long before he turned up. The labyrinth was his domain and he didn't like anyone coming to play there. The older kids in the Demo had told us he set wolf traps to catch children playing close to his cars. So we always looked carefully where we put our feet.

Whenever the owner heard us, he would arrive yelling "What's all this?" and we would have to scram before we got caught, climbing back up the slope, hanging onto the roots, fighting the fear that made breathing difficult, and run a long, long way from the shouts of "What's all this?" Being fat and heavy, the guy couldn't climb very far up the wall of sand.

One day, Sam grabbed hold of a too-slender root, and it broke. He fell straight down, landing a few inches from the huge hands that were trying to catch him. He leapt like a cat, I caught him by his sleeve, and we barely made it out of there. Once up top, we laughed in fright. We went to see Monica beneath the ivy to tell her about it. She laughed too, but warned us not to have any hassle with him. She said it just like that, in her voice that sounded like an old car horn, and with her beachy scent: "You know, kiddies, there are people you shouldn't approach. You'll learn that. There are people who'll darken your skies, who'll steal your joy, who'll sit on your shoulders to stop you flying free. He is one such person. Stay well away from people like that." I giggled, imagining the owner of the wrecking yard sitting on Sam's shoulders. Then we left for the Demo because we heard the music—Tchaikovsky's "Flower Waltz"—coming from the ice-cream man's truck, bang on time, as he was every evening. We went to ask our father for some money.

Sam always had two scoops, vanilla and strawberry. I chose chocolate and stracciatella, with whipped cream, even though whipped cream was forbidden: my father didn't approve, I don't know why. So I quickly gulped it down before we went home. It was a secret I shared with my little brother and the nice man in the truck. He was very old; he was bald, tall, and slender; and he wore a brown velvet suit. He would always tell us, in his gravelly voice and with a gleam in his eyes, "Eat it fast before it melts, kiddos, because it's sunny and windy, and there's nothing worse for ice cream."

ONE SUMMER EVENING, my mother had made peaches stuffed with tuna, which we ate on the blue stone terrace overlooking the garden. My father had already left the table to settle down in front of the TV with his bottle of Glenfiddich. He disliked spending time with us. I think nobody in our family liked gathering for the evening meal, but my father imposed this ritual upon us, as much as he imposed it upon himself. Because that's how things were. A family takes its meals together, whether they enjoy it or not. That's what we saw on TV. Except that people seemed happy on TV, particularly in the commercials. They chatted, they laughed. They were beautiful and loved each other. Family time was sold as a reward. Along with Ferrero Rocher, it was supposed to be the treat you were entitled to after long hours working in the office or at school. Our own family meals seemed more like a punishment, a big glass of piss we had to drink daily. Each evening proceeded according to a ritual that bordered on the sacred. My father would watch the TV news, explaining each subject to my mother—on the principle that she was incapable of comprehending the slightest bit of information without his enlightenment. The TV news was important to my father. Commenting on the news gave him the impression of having a role to play in it. As if the world depended upon his reflections in order to progress in the proper manner. When the end credits boomed out, my mother would yell: "Dinner's ready!" My father would leave the TV on, and everyone would sit down to eat in silence. When he got up to return to his couch, we felt something like a liberation. That evening, too, like all the others.

Sam and I had left the table to go play in the garden. The sun caressed the fading day with a light that bore the sweet scent of caramelized honey. In the hallway, my mother was cleaning Coco's cage. I had tried to tell my mother that it was cruel keeping a parakeet in a cage. Especially as the garden was full of them—which was a problem, in fact, because the parakeets ate the food of the little birds such as the sparrows and chickadees; not to mention our cherries, which they devoured before they had time to ripen on the tree. The reason we had parakeets around was that there had once been a small zoo several miles from the Demo. But it went bust when an amusement park opened nearby and drew all its visitors away. Most of the animals were sold to other zoos, but nobody gave a damn about the parakeets, and transporting them would have cost too much. So the director simply opened their cage. Perhaps he thought they'd die of cold. But they didn't. On the contrary, they adapted, built nests, and had young. They always moved as a group, forming big green clouds that flew across the sky. It was pretty. Noisy but pretty.

I didn't understand why that poor Coco had to stay in a cage and watch the others having fun without her. My mother said that it wasn't the same, that she'd come from a store, that she wasn't used to it. But still.

So my mother was cleaning Coco's cage. It was "Flower Waltz" and ice-cream time. The truck had stopped alongside our house, by the hedge. The old ice-cream man was there, a dozen children chirruping around him. Monica had told me that he wasn't like the owner of the car boneyard, he was kind. When she had talked about him, I had seen something strange in her eyes. I told myself that since they were both old, perhaps there had been something between them once. Perhaps a beautiful love story thwarted by old family feuds—I was reading quite a lot of Harlequin books at the time.

When the ice-cream man handed Sam his vanilla and strawberry ice cream, I looked at his hands. There's something reassuring about old people's hands. As I imagined how their delicate, elaborate mechanism had functioned and obeyed this fellow without him thinking about it, for such a long time, and as I thought about the tons of ice creams they had made, without ever letting him down, it gave me faith in something I couldn't define. It was reassuring. The hands were beautiful too, the skin so thin over the tendons they were almost bare, the blue veins like streams.

He looked at me, eyes twinkling:

"And for you, my little darling?"

It was my turn. I'd been repeating the line in my head for the past five minutes. I didn't like to improvise when ordering an ice cream, I don't know why. There had to be someone in line ahead of me, giving me time to choose what I wanted and to put together my sentence. So it would come out right, with no hesitation. We were the last that day, the rest of the kids having had their ice cream and left already.

"Chocolate and stracciatella in a cone with whipped cream, please sir."

"With whipped cream, my little lady! But of course ..."

He winked as he pronounced the words *whipped cream* to let me know it was still our little secret. Then his hands, his two faithful dogs, set to work, repeating their little dance for the hundred-thousandth time. The cone, the ice-cream scoop, one scoop of chocolate, the tub of warm water, one scoop of stracciatella, then the siphon, a real siphon, containing homemade whipped cream.

The old man leaned forward to put a pretty whirl of cream on top of my two scoops. His blue eyes were open wide, tightly focused on the cloudy spiral, the siphon against his cheek, the movement gracious, precise. His hand so close to his face. Just when he had reached the summit of the little cream mountain, right when his finger was preparing to ease off and he was about to straighten up, the siphon exploded. *BANG!*

I remember the sound. It was the sound that petrified me first. It slammed into each wall of the Demo. My heart skipped two beats. It must have been heard as far as the depths of Little Gallows Wood, as far as Monica's house.

Then I saw the kind old man's face. The siphon had smashed into it like a car through the front of a house. Half of it was missing. His bald head remained intact, but his face was a mash of meat and bone. A single eye hung in its socket. I took it all in. I had time. The eye looked surprised. The old man stayed standing for a couple of seconds, as if his body needed time to realize that it now had mincemeat for a face. Then it crumpled.

It seemed like a joke. I could even hear laughter. Not real laughter, and not coming from me. I think it was death. Or fate. Or something like that. Something much bigger than myself. Some supernatural force that decides everything and that was in a mischievous mood that day, and so decided to have a little fun with the old man's face.

I don't remember much after that. I screamed. People came. They screamed too. My father came. Sam stood motionless, his big eyes open wide, his little mouth agape, clutching his cone of vanilla and strawberry ice cream. A man puked up melon with Parma ham. The ambulance arrived, then the hearse.

* * *

My father took us home, in silence, then returned to his seat in front of the TV. My mother gave the floor by Coco's cage a quick sweep. I took Sam's hand and led him to the goat pen. He followed me like a sleepwalker, staring straight ahead, mouth half-open.

It all seemed unreal—the garden, the swimming pool, the rosemary, the night that was falling—or rather it seemed tinged with a new reality, the savage reality of flesh and blood, of pain, and the march of time, linear and relentless. But above all, it was the reality of that force I heard laughing as the old man's body crumpled to the floor. That laughter which was neither within me nor outside me. That laughter which was everywhere, in everything, as was that force. It could find me wherever. No place to hide. And if I couldn't hide, then nothing existed. Nothing but blood and terror.

I wanted to go see the goats because I hoped their ruminant indifference would pull me back to reality and that this would reassure me. The three of them were grazing in their pen. A bunch of parakeets perched on the branches of the cherry tree. Nothing made sense anymore. My reality had dissolved into a vertiginous void from which I saw no way out. A void so palpable I could feel its walls, its floor, and its ceiling tightening around me. I felt stifled by a primitive panic. I would have liked someone—an adult—to take me by the hand and put me to bed. Reposition the markers of my existence. Tell me there'd be a tomorrow after this day, and then another day after that, and that my life would eventually look like it had before. That the blood and the terror would dissipate.

But nobody came.

The parakeets ate the still-green cherries. Sam maintained his wide-eyed stare, mouth agape, little fist clutching the ice-cream cone covered with melted vanilla and strawberry. I told myself that if nobody was going to put me to bed, I could at least do that for Sam. I would have liked to talk to him, to tell him something reassuring, but I was unable. Panic hadn't loosened its grip around my throat. I took him to my room and we both got into my bed. My window overlooked the garden, the goats, and the wood. The wind set the shadow of an oak tree dancing on the wooden floor. I couldn't sleep. At one point I heard my mother coming upstairs. Then my father, an hour later. They never came up together, but they still shared the same bed. I imagined this must have been part of the "normal family" package, like the meals. I wondered sometimes whether there were moments of tenderness between them. Like there were between

Sam and me. I wished it for them, without much conviction. I couldn't imagine a life without tenderness, particularly on a night like this.

I watched each minute chasing the last on my clock radio. They seemed to get longer and longer. I felt like puking. But I didn't want to get up and risk waking Sam if he'd been fortunate enough to fall asleep. His back was toward me, so I couldn't see his eyes.

Around five in the morning, something called me outside, a kind of intuition. I went down into the garden. The darkness terrified me even more than usual. I imagined there were creatures crouched in the shadows ready to gnaw off my face—the way the ice-cream man's had been. I went as far as the goat pen. Nutmeg was standing a little apart from the others. A long, viscous thread hung beneath her tail.

I WENT BACK up to my room.

"Sam, the babies have come." Those words, the first I had uttered since ordering my ice cream with whipped cream, sounded quite odd, as if they had come from a vanished world. Sam didn't react.

I went to wake my mother, who came downstairs, quite beside herself. I don't know how to describe an overexcited amoeba; it's all messy and clumsy, and it talks fast and loud, dashing all over the place: "Warm water, camphor-alcohol, Betadine, towels, a wheelbarrow, straw ..."

I pulled Sam out of my bed so he could come see. By the time we got down there, two little hooves had already appeared. Then a muzzle. Nutmeg pushed, bleated, pushed, bleated, pushed. It looked painful. And hard too. Then, all of a sudden, the kid slid out of her body. Nutmeg began pushing again, and bleating, pushing, bleating, pushing. There was a strange smell. A warm smell of body and guts. A second baby appeared. Nutmeg got up and, while she was licking her kids, a large brownish slimy mass spurted out of her and splatted on the ground. Nutmeg turned and began to eat the brownish mass. The warm smell had grown stronger. It seemed to emanate from Nutmeg's belly to fill the whole of the earth's atmosphere. I wondered how such a small goat could contain so much smell.

My mother got down on all fours and began to hug and kiss the baby goats. Two males. She rubbed her face all over their sticky little bodies. Then, still on all fours, she turned to us, her face smeared with residue from the amniotic sac.

"They will be called Cumin and Paprika."

* * *

It was hot the following days. White sun pouring from an empty sky.

My father was on edge. He came home from work with furrowed brows. I had noticed before that he was like that when he hadn't been hunting for a long while. He slammed the front door, chucked down his keys and briefcase, then began to search for a reason to spew all his rage. He went from room to room, scrutinizing everything in the house, the floor, the furniture, my mother, Coco, Sam, me. Sniffing out a scent. Times like those, we knew it was best to vanish to our bedrooms. My mother couldn't, she had to prepare the meal. Sometimes he settled for merely grumbling before going to sit in front of the TV. This could go on for several days. Brewing. And then, as always, he finally found it.

"What's that?"

He asked the question quite gently, and very quietly. My mother knew that whatever she said it wouldn't go well. But she answered anyway.

"Macaroni with ham and cheese."

"I know it's macaroni with ham and cheese."

He was still speaking very softly.

"Why did you make macaroni with ham and cheese?"

And the longer he spoke in this gentle

voice, the more dreadful his building rage would be. This was the scariest moment for my mother, I think, when she knew it was going to come, that he was examining her, savoring her fear, taking his time. He acted as if it all depended on her answer. This was the game. But she lost every time.

"Well, everyone likes macaroni with—"

"EVERYONE? WHO IS THIS 'EVERYONE'?"

And so it began. The best she could hope for was that my father's anger would be expended in the yelling—which was in fact more like a roar. His voice detonated from his throat to devour my mother, ripping her to shreds, annihilating her. And my mother was OK with that. Annihilation. If the roaring didn't suffice, his fists were ready to help out, until my father's rage was totally spent. My mother always ended up on the floor, motionless. Like an empty pillowcase. After that, we knew we had a few weeks of calm ahead.

* * *

I don't think my father liked his job. He was an accountant at the amusement park that had made the little zoo go bust. "The big eat the small," he would say. It seemed to amuse him. "The big eat the small." Personally, I thought it was amazing to work in an amusement park. When I set off for school each morning, I said to myself: "My father's going to spend his day at the amusement park."

My mother didn't work. She looked after her goats, her garden, Coco, and us. She couldn't care less about having her own money, as long as her credit card worked. Emptiness never seemed to bother my mother. Nor the absence of love.

The ice-cream man's truck remained parked in front of our house for several days. I asked myself all sorts of questions. Who's going to clean it? And once it's been cleaned, what happens to the bucket full of water, soap, blood, bone fragments, and bits of brain? Will they pour it on the old man's grave so that all the pieces of him stay together? Has the ice cream in the fridges melted? And if it hasn't melted, will someone eat it? Can the police put someone in prison for asking for whipped cream? Will they tell my father?

At home, we never talked about the death of the old ice-cream man. Maybe my parents considered that the best response was to act as if nothing had happened. Or maybe they told themselves that the birth of the baby goats had made us forget the mincemeat face. But in fact, I think they had simply not given it any thought.

Sam remained silent for three whole days. I didn't dare look in his big green eyes because I was sure that in them I would see, projected on a continuous loop, the film of that exploding face. He didn't eat anything either. His fish and mashed potato grew cold on the plate. I tried to entertain him. He followed me around like a docile robot, but he was dead inside.

We went to see Monica. Something quivered beneath the skin on her neck when she learned what had happened to the ice-cream man. She looked at Sam. I hoped she'd do something for him, that she'd take out a cauldron, a magic wand, or an old spell book. But she just stroked his cheek.

THE WARM ODOR from Nutmeg's belly still lingered. I think it lingered more in my head really, but my abiding memory of the summer was that persistent icky scent, which clung to me even in my dreams. It was July and yet the nights seemed darker and colder than in winter.

Sam came to snuggle in my bed every night. With my nose buried in his hair, I could almost hear his nightmares. I would have given everything I had to turn back time and go back to that moment where I had asked for the ice cream. I imagined the scene a thousand times: "Chocolate and stracciatella in a cone, please sir," I say to the ice-cream man; "No whipped cream today, my little lady?" he asks; "No thanks, sir," I reply. And my planet is not sucked into a black hole. And the old man's face does not explode in front of my little brother and my home. And I continue to hear the "Flower Waltz" the next day and the day after, and the story ends there. And Sam smiles.

* * *

I remembered a film I'd once seen, in which a crazy scientist invents a machine to go back in time. He uses a car all cobbled together, with wires everywhere, and he has to drive really fast but he manages it. I decided that I, too, would invent a machine and travel through time and sort everything out.

From that moment on, I saw my life as a flawed offshoot of reality, a draft version intended to be rewritten. It made everything seem more bearable. I told myself that until such time as the machine was ready and I could turn back the clock, I would have to coax my little brother out of his silence.

I took him to the labyrinth, straight to the Boom-a-roller. "Sit down." He obediently sat. I took my place at the wheel and began bouncing up and down on the seat with all my strength, shaking the car like never before. "Boom-a-rollerrrrr! Boom-a-rollerrrrr! Boom-a-rollerrrrr! C'mon, Sam! Boom-a-rollerrrrr!" He just sat there, unresponsive, his big green eyes quite empty. He looked so tired. Luckily the owner didn't hear us, because in the state Sam was in he would have let himself be caught without a fight.

At home, I made new puppets, invented new stories. My little audience of one sat in front of me as I told him of princesses who tripped over their dresses, farting prince charmings, and hiccoughing dragons ... Eventually, without really knowing why, I led him into the carcass room. My father was at work and my mother had gone out for some groceries. When we entered the room, I felt the hyena's eyes on me. I carefully avoided meeting her gaze.

And at that moment, I understood. It swooped on me like a hungry beast, slashing my back with its claws. The laughter I'd heard when the old man's face exploded, it came from her. That thing I couldn't quite discern, was living inside the hyena. Her stuffed body was a monster's lair. Death resided within our home, and was scrutinizing me through her glass eyes, its gaze boring into the back of my neck as it savored my little brother's sweet scent.

Sam let go of my hand and turned toward the creature. He approached and placed his fingers on the rigid muzzle. I didn't dare move a muscle. The hyena was going to awaken and devour him. Sam fell to his knees, his lips quivering. He stroked the dead fur and put his arms round the beast's neck, his little face so close to the huge jaw. Then he began to sob, his sparrow-like body shaken by floods of terror. The horror burst and poured down his cheeks, like from an abscess that had taken its time to ripen. I realized that this boded well, that something was circulating in him anew, that his internal mechanism was working again.

* * *

A few days later, the ice-cream man was replaced by another one, and the "Flower Waltz" returned. Every evening, the mincemeat face loomed in my mind. Every evening, I saw something snap in my little brother's eyes. That music struck at a part deep within him, the central component of his joy-production process, destroying it a little more each day, rendering it ever more ir-reparable. And every evening I told myself that it was no big deal, that I was just in the flawed offshoot of my life, that it was all in-tended to be rewritten.

Whenever the ice-cream truck came, I tried to be close to Sam. I could clearly see how his entire little body shivered as soon as he heard the music.

One evening, I couldn't find Sam in his bedroom, or in mine, or in the garden. So I crept into the carcass room, without a sound because my father was in the living room. I found Sam in there, sitting by the hyena. He was whispering into her big ears. I didn't hear what he was saying to her. When he noticed my presence, he gave me an odd look. I felt as if it was the hyena look-ing at me. What if the shock of the explod-ing cream siphon had opened a breach into Sam's head? What if the hyena had taken advantage of this breach to go and live within my little brother? Or inject something evil into him? That look I saw on Sam's face, it wasn't him. It smacked of blood and death. It reminded me that the beast was on the prowl and that it slept inside my home. And I realized it now resided within Sam.

My parents saw nothing. My father was too busy delivering his TV commentary to my mother, and she was too busy being frightened of him.

I HAD TO begin building this machine to go back in time as soon as possible. I went to see Monica, certain she could help me.

Her house was still there, down in the claw mark, with the sun's hand upon it. She opened the door, wearing one of her long dresses—all bright colors, flowers, and butterflies. Inside, there was that familiar cinnamon smell. I went in and sat down on the banquette covered with a sheepskin. It was like the ivory in the carcass room, soft with something powerful behind, as if the animal's spirit still dwelled inside and could feel my caresses.

Monica gave me an apple juice. In her face, too, something was missing since the death of the ice-cream man. I didn't dare tell her it was my fault, that it was I who had asked for whipped cream. Nobody must ever know that. I told her about Sam and my time-travel idea.

"In the film, you see, there's this car and it needs a vast amount of energy. They use plutonium. And when they don't have any plutonium, they make use of lightning. I can get hold of the car and cobble it together a bit, but I don't know how to create lightning. Do you know if it's possible to bring on a storm?"

She smiled slightly, her sadness wandering off outside for a while.

"Yes, I think it's possible. It won't be easy, far from it, it'll take a lot of work, but I think it's possible. I've already heard of it, at any rate. It's a combination of science and magic. I'll take care of the storm if you like. For the science part, you'll just have to learn as you go, but you'll get there if you really want to. It will take time, more than you think, but you'll get there. Like Marie Curie."

I pinched my lips together.

"Shit, you don't know who Marie Curie is? What do they do with you at school all day? Marie Curie, for fuck's sake! C'mon! Real name: Maria Salomea Skłodowska. She became Curie when she married Pierre Curie. First woman to receive the Nobel Prize. The one and only woman in the history of the Nobels to receive two: the Nobel Prize in Physics with her husband, in 1903, for their research on radiation; then, after Pierre died, *boom!* another Nobel, but in chemistry this time, in 1911, for her work on polonium and radium. It was she who discovered these two elements. Polonium she named as a homage to her country of origin. You've never seen a periodic table either, I bet?"

I shook my head.

"Dear me … She worked like a maniac all her life. Have you ever broken something? An arm? A leg?"

"Yes, my arm when I was seven."

"Right. Did they x-ray you to see the fracture?"

"Yes."

"Thank you, Marie Curie."

"You think she could help me? Where does she live?"

"Ah, no. She died. From radiation. But what I mean is that if you work really hard at something, you can get there."

"So if I cobble together a car, you'll help me with the storm?"

"Cross my heart."

* * *

I returned home reassured: I had a solution and I was not alone. So I started the next day. I got hold of all the documentation I could find on Marie Curie, as well as the *Back to the Future* trilogy. I knew it would take time, but every day Sam's state called me to my duty.

Summer ended and the school year passed, bland and boring, as always. Every moment of my free time was spent perfecting my plan.

THE FOLLOWING SUMMER arrived. Sam's state hadn't improved. The emptiness in his eyes had gradually filled with something incandescent, pointed, and sharp-edged. Whatever was living inside the hyena had slowly migrated into my little brother's head. A colony of wild beasts had set up residence there, feeding off slivers of his brain. This teeming army proliferated, burning the primeval forests and turning them into dark, swampy landscapes.

I loved him. And I was going to fix it all. Nothing could stop me, even if he no longer played with me, even if his laughter became as ghastly as acid rain on a field of poppies. I loved him like a mother loves a sick child. His birthday was September 26. I decided that everything should be ready by that day.

* * *

My father had just returned from a hunting trip in the Himalayas. He had brought back the head of a brown bear, which he hung on his wall of trophies—having taken down several stag antlers to make room. The bear's pelt, he had draped over his couch and he slumped on it every night to watch TV. He had been gone three weeks and we experienced his absence as a relief.

In the weeks before he left, he had been edgy like never before. We were having dinner one evening and I knew that he was going to fly into a rage. All four of us knew it. For days he had been coming home from work and sniffing around, in every nook, as tense as a coiled spring. Sam and I hid away in our rooms, convinced he was going to explode. But he didn't. And his edginess mounted, like pressurized propane.

So we were having dinner that evening. Everyone was eating in silence, with precise, measured movements. Nobody wanted to be responsible for the spark that would cause the explosion. The only sounds (which filled the room) came from my father: from his jaws as they chewed huge chunks of meat; and from his short, husky breaths. The beans and mash on his plate looked like two atolls lost in a bloody sea. I forced myself to eat so as not to stand out, but my stomach was all in knots. I watched him out of the corner of my eye, alert to the coming cataclysm.

He put his cutlery down. In a barely audible whisper, he said, "Is that what you call 'bloody'?" My mother turned so pale you'd have thought all her blood had poured onto my father's plate. She said nothing. There was no good answer to that question.

My father was insistent: "Well?"

"There's a lot of blood on your plate," she murmured.

"So, you're happy with yourself?" he snarled between his teeth.

My mother closed her eyes. This was it. He picked up his plate in his two monstrous fists and smashed it against the table.

"WHO THE HELL DO YOU THINK YOU ARE?!"

He grabbed my mother by her hair and squashed her face into the mashed potato and broken china.

"WHO DO YOU THINK YOU ARE? YOU THINK YOU'RE SOMETHING? YOU'RE NOTHING! NOTHING!"

My mother whined in pain. She didn't beg, she didn't struggle, she knew there was no point. All I could see of her deformed face, squashed by my father's hand, was her mouth twisted in terror. All three of us knew that this time would be worse than all the others. Sam and I remained frozen. We didn't think to go upstairs: our father's rages usually exploded *after* dinner, rather than during, so we were rarely spectators.

He pulled my mother's head up by her hair, then slammed it several times onto the same spot on the table, into the remains of the plate. I could no longer tell if the blood was from the steak or from my mother. Then I reminded myself that none of this mattered because I was going to travel back in time and delete it all. None of this would exist anymore in my new life.

When my father had calmed down, I took Sam's hand and we went up to my room. We hid beneath my quilt. I told him we were inside an ostrich's egg and that we were playing hide-and-go-seek with Monica. That this was all just a game, only a game. A game.

Two days later my father left to go hunting in the Himalayas and we could breathe freely again.

A FEW DAYS after our father got back, Sam and I tagged along with our mother when she went shopping. We dropped by the pet store because she needed vitamin powder for the goats. It was a huge warehouse in which you could find all kinds of things, for both pets and livestock. My mother liked chatting with the guy there. He was a farmer's son and knew everything about animals. So Sam and I would go and play on the straw bales. They were stacked pretty high, like a fortress you had to climb. You just needed to watch out for the holes. The guy said that a child in his family once died after falling down a hole between the bales.

They were giving away some puppies that day—the litter of the warehouse's broken-coated Jack Russell. I thought she looked like an old toothbrush. I asked my mother if we could take one. She agreed, of course, but it was up to my father to decide.

I went to see him that very evening, in the living room. He was in a calm mood, having recently shot his bear.

From time to time—not often—he would put some music on instead of watching TV: Claude François. Such was the case that evening. I approached the couch without making any noise, because noise was something my father couldn't stand. He really was extremely calm, sitting perfectly straight, hands on his knees, motionless. By that time of day, nearly all the outside light had disappeared from the room. His face was half-swallowed by the twilight. Claude François was singing "Le téléphone pleure." *Words expire in the receiver. The telephone weeps. Don't hang up.* There was a strange glint on my father's cheek. I sat down close to him on the couch.

"Dad?"

He started slightly, wiped away the glint with his hand, then grunted, but not like usual. A softer kind of grunt.

I often wondered why he cried. Particularly to that song—in which a man talks on the phone with a little girl who doesn't know he's her dad. I knew he had never known his own father, but no one had told me why. Was he dead? Had he abandoned my dad? Had the fact he had a son been kept from him? Whatever the reason, this absence seemed to have gnawed a hole in my father's chest, just beneath his shirt. This hole sucked in anything that got too close, and crushed it. That was why he had never taken me in his arms. I understood, and didn't resent him for it.

"Dad, we were at the pet store before, and they had puppies and I wanted to know if I could have one."

He looked at me. He seemed tired, as if he had just lost a battle.

"Sure, sweetie."

Sweetie. I thought my heart would burst. Sweetie. My father had called me "sweetie." That little word flashed in my mind like a firefly, before slipping away somewhere deep in my chest. Its light glowed there for several days. The following morning, my mother took us to collect the puppy. Sam stroked each one in turn. He didn't smile, but it seemed to do him good, the feel of those soft, warm, little balls between his hands. "You pick the puppy," I said to him, "and I'll pick the name. OK?"

"This one." He lifted the puppy that was on his knees. "That's a female," the pet-store guy said. "She'll be called Curie," I announced, "like Marie Curie." I thought it would bring me luck. That perhaps it would attract the attention of Marie Curie, up there in heaven—if heaven existed—and that she would give me a hand.

When we got home, I took Sam and Curie to the labyrinth of broken cars. Partly to show Curie around, but also because I had to choose the car I'd use to make my machine to go back in time.

* * *

As we crossed the cornfield, we ran into some kids from the Demo. Derek's gang. I didn't like those guys much. Fighting was all that interested them. It's not that I had a particular interest in Barbie dolls and skipping ropes, I liked to fight too; but only play fighting, to see who was the strongest, without hurting each other. These kids bit and they punched hard, right in the gut, Derek above all. He had a weird scar by his mouth that gave him a feral grimace, like a grin, even when he was enraged. And he was always enraged, with an anger that had nested itself deep in his knotted blond hair; not to mention that Derek and his gang were nasty to Sam because he was little. So we tried to avoid them whenever we could.

They saw us from afar and Derek called out, "Hey, rich kids!"

They only called us that because our house was a little bigger than the others in the Demo. And we had an inflatable swimming pool. We pretended we hadn't heard them and we ran all the way to the labyrinth. Loads of new cars had arrived and it took me all afternoon to reassure them. Not only because there were so many, but also because Sam didn't want to help me. He stayed sat by himself drawing shapes in the sand with a stick.

I saw a shell that seemed in a decent state: a pretty red car that looked a little like the Doc's DeLorean. I figured it had died of old age, rather than a crash.

* * *

Now I needed to go see Monica again.

THE DAY AFTER Curie's arrival, my mother returned from the hardware store all proud. She had had an identification tag made for the puppy. My mother was always performing small kindnesses for the animals. I looked at the little metal roundel, which had our phone number engraved on one side and "Curry" on the other.

I had never felt much for my mother, other than deep compassion. But the moment my eyes deciphered those five letters, that compassion instantly dissolved into a puddle of dark, stinking disdain.

I decided to rename the puppy Skłodowska—I thought it might please Marie Curie even more if I gave her maiden name to my dog. But "Skłodowska" was a bit of a mouthful. So to simplify things, I shortened it to Dovka. This amused my father and he began calling her Vodka. I chucked the tag away, of course, and told my parents that Dovka had lost it.

* * *

Now that I more or less understood what I had to do with the car to turn it into a machine for going back in time, I went to see Monica again.

When I got to her house, she was sitting outside on a thick tree trunk, in her ray of sunlight, wrapped in a colorful crocheted plaid, making a vase on a potter's wheel. I watched her for a few moments without being seen. Monica's slender, muscular arms, spotted with freckles, her coppery skin smelling of cardamom, and that gaze of an Amerindian priestess, must have filled entire mental institutions with despairing lovers.

She greeted me as I approached, her voice resonant of the open sea.

"Hey! Been a while since we last saw you round these parts! How's it going, kid?"

I told her everything I had learned about time travel, and my goal of September 26.

After reading a biography of Marie Curie, I realized that I wanted to become like her. Someone not afraid of taking their place in the world, of playing a role and making a contribution to scientific progress. She laughed. "Well, well, well, my darling!" I asked her if she had gotten anywhere with her storm-conjuring task. She told me she was going to need an object.

"Something irreplaceable. It doesn't necessarily have to be an expensive object, but it must be irreplaceable. Something that's precious to you or to someone you love. The higher the object's sentimental value, the stronger the magic will be, and the greater the chance of it working. Come back and see me when you've got it. Another thing, I can only bring on a storm during the night of a full moon."

The idea came to me instantly. I knew the perfect object. An icy shiver ran up the back of my neck. It was madness, but it was the only solution.

"I'll come back and see you with the object when the car's ready, in late summer."

I set off back home. I felt like taking Dovka for a walk in the fields. Maybe Sam would want to come with me. He was spending most of his time on his Game Boy, but sometimes he still agreed to come play hide-and-go-seek with me in the corn fields. The large, sharp leaves would graze our cheeks and our arms, and in the evening my skin would be burning and I'd promise myself never to do it again.

Dovka wasn't to be found in the garden when I got back home. I went to have a look on her cushion in the living room, since she still slept a lot, being quite young. She wasn't there either. I asked my mother, but she had just returned from doing the shopping and hadn't seen Dovka. Her face still bore the marks of my father's fit of rage— the longest to heal was a deep gash just beneath her right eye. She helped me look. We searched the house, the garden, and the goat pen, but there was no trace of Dovka. Sam hadn't seen her either. He was with the hyena again. My mother told him off: he wasn't allowed to be there, and if our father found out …

Panic began to tighten its large hand around my throat, just like the night the ice-cream man died. Why hadn't I taken

Dovka with me to go see Monica?

We had to widen the search. If she wasn't in the house, she couldn't have gone far. Somewhere around the Demo or the woods. But we had to be quick. My mother went off to the woods, Sam and I out into the Demo. I thought my mom might come across Monica, and, if so, I would have really liked to be there to see it. But I had to focus on the urgent matter at hand.

It was oppressively hot. One of those scorching days that ends in a sky the color of bitumen and a storm loaded with the scent of burning asphalt. Sam and I went calling at all the houses. I was happy he'd agreed to help me. We went from door to door, repeating the same speech, like little sales reps. Folks were generally nice. Particularly this one young couple. A tall feather of a girl opened the door, slim and sweet, and smelling of modeling clay, with a tiny baby in her arms. She called to her fiancé, a guy who was even taller than her, bare-chested, tattooed, and very muscular. "He's a karate champion," said Feather Girl, proud and lovestruck. She thought Sam and I were "so beautiful and so well-brought-up." They gave us some orange juice. I saw that Sam was looking at the baby with an attentiveness I'd not seen in him for a long time. The karate champion appeared genuinely concerned for Dovka. I couldn't stop myself studying the topography of that chest, the contours of the muscles under the skin, the bulging veins ... It put me in mind of a wild horse. A powerful animal, twitchy with energy, yet affectionate. I wanted him to wrap his arms around me. Something warm swelled in my belly. I straightaway knew that this swelling was the kind to divert me from my objectives, so I smothered it by contracting my abdominals as hard as I could. We finished our orange juice, thanked them, said goodbye, and continued our inquiries.

* * *

Our hopes faded as we went from one ugly house to the next. I started imagining my poor doggie squished by the side of a country road or eaten by a fox.

The thing about all these identical houses was that they were, in actual fact, no such thing. Identical, that is. Not in the slightest. The architecture was the same, a sort of gray polypropylene container pierced with a few scarce windows and topped with a tiled roof. But given such similarity, every difference stood out. The inhabitants' personalities, their lifestyles, exuded from the simplest curtain, flowerpot, or lampshade. Some houses seemed to scream their occupants' solitude and the vertiginous inconsistency of their existences. Like that old lady's, whose lawn was populated by china creatures: gnomes, fawns, rabbits.

We got to a house that looked even grayer than the rest. I knew it. It was where Derek lived. An old tire lay in the yellowing grass of the small garden alongside a faded red plastic sandpit in the shape of a shell. Near the door, the remains of what must have been a flat-pack wardrobe lay rotting like the swollen carcass of a drowned woman on a riverbank. I rang the doorbell, in spite of the instinctive fear that was starting to gnaw at my gut. From behind the door a voice roared:

"What is it?!"

"Hello sir, we're looking for our little dog

who's gone missing. Might you have seen her?"

The door opened on a guy in sweatpants and top, stinking of a mixture of alcohol, tobacco, and urine. One part of his brain attempted to look us up and down, while the other appeared to be struggling fiercely to keep his body upright. In one of his hands, folded against his chest, he held Dovka.

Seeing Sam and me, the dog started yapping and wriggling. The man lurched.

"Oh! You've found her! Thank you sir!"

At that, the guy curled his lip strangely, narrowed his eyes a little, and said:

"Tell yer father I'll return the mutt if he lets us swim in yer pool, me and my kid."

He leaned aside to reveal Derek who was standing six feet behind him in the hallway. The guy's lolling eyes beneath their puffy eyelids stayed fixed on Sam and me. But now his cerebral faculties were entirely focused on preventing his body from collapsing. Dovka whined, struggling harder and harder. It struck me that it must be true torture to have a dog's sense of smell in this house. I already had trouble breathing. A small handful of the guy's neurons seemed to detach from the fight against gravity to activate an arm muscle, which closed the door. I didn't dare look at Sam. Because I knew that if my gaze met his, the tears I'd been holding back with all my might would start to flow. And I didn't want him to see me cry. Not out of fear that my distress would be contagious, but because I was worried my tears would feed the teeming vermin in his head.

We set off home, in silence. Once back, I explained the problem to my mother. She seemed a little fazed, her eyes quivered in their sockets for a few moments, then she said:

"You'll have to discuss it with your father when he gets back."

I imagined Dovka's ordeal. It was out of the question to leave her there until my father returned. I thought back to the karate champion and his wild-horse of a body. The warm thing in my belly swelled again, but stronger than the first time. I let it happen because I felt that, now, there was no contradiction between this swelling and my objective of getting Dovka out of there at all costs.

I set off again. Sam came with me. I rang the bell and Feather Girl answered the door, a little surprised. The Champion listened to our tale. His jaw tightened, making a lovely shape just above his ears. He looked like Clark Kent when he turns into Superman, his superhero instinct awakened. Without bothering to even put on a T-shirt, the Champion told us to follow him, and he headed straight for that house even grayer than the rest. The Champion banged on the door. Derek opened, and before he had time to realize what was happening, the Champion had shoved him out of the way and was striding into the house. I followed. The kid's father was flopped on an old couch that must have housed an entire ecosystem of parasites and mold. Dovka was asleep in his arms. The Champion delicately picked the puppy up and returned her to me. The guy opened one eye, just in time to see the Champion's fist slam into his jaw. "You piece of shit!" went the Champion again and again and again, hitting the guy like he was a sandbag. Each blow made a dull thud. Derek jumped on the flexed arm—as hard and as powerful as the business end of a percussion drill—and tried to bite it. The Champion grabbed him with his other arm and sent him flying across the room.

When he had finished venting his rage on the guy, he looked at his bloody fist with a perplexed air, as if wondering if it were really his. The guy lay embedded in his couch, like a rabbit in the asphalt of a country road. Blood ran from his mouth to mingle with the other stains on his T-shirt. I saw in Sam's eyes the vermin rejoicing at this show, and they set to copulating again, colonizing and laying waste to the scant lands that still remained fertile and alive in my little brother's head. "Thank you sir," I said to the Champion, who smiled as he stroked Dovka's head. "No worries, sweetie," he said. In a corner of the room, Derek, terrorized, didn't dare move.

* * *

On the way home, the ice-cream truck passed, playing the "Flower Waltz." I took Sam's hand. It was cold and stiff like a dead bird. The hyena laughed as she tore my guts to shreds.

ACCORDING TO MY book *The Scientist's Companion*, of the various theories regarding time travel, the most plausible was the "wormhole" theory. Basically, you needed to create a wormhole, which would allow you to move from one space-time to another. And to create a wormhole, you needed to accelerate particles with phenomenal energy.

Among the odds and ends lying about in the car boneyard, I found an old microwave, which I connected to the car's battery. If my theory was correct, I would just have to program the microwave to the date and time of the ice-cream man's death, start the car and bring on the storm, all on the night of a full moon. It only remained to supply Monica with the object she required. The next full moon would be August 29. I knew I'd be ready.

My memory of the days following Dov-ka's kidnapping was of something like a long drawn-out death. It was as if that summer had been struck by an aggressive cancer before it was even born. As I waited for August 29, the flower-filled garden seemed like a hospital room.

Sam spent more and more time in the carcass room talking to the hyena. The vermin in his head had seized control. Even his face appeared changed. His eyes had sunk in their sockets, and his face seemed to have swollen from the proliferation of parasites eating away at his brain. Yet I was sure that somewhere, in the far reaches of his soul, there existed a bastion of resistance, one small village of indomitable Gauls still holding out against the invaders. I was sure of this because every night he slipped into my bed. He said nothing, but he snuggled up just a couple of inches from me. I could hear his tears hitting the mattress like tiny falling bodies and I realized that the noise of his tears was the echo of the Gaulish village in outcry, far away, once the vermin had fallen asleep. I took him in my arms, even if something inside of me was saying that his body against mine, his seven years against my eleven, was starting to become weird. But I couldn't care less. I hoped that, through induction, I could feed his pocket of resistance. I imagined airplanes dropping crates of food to a population of skinny but robust men, women, and children. A united and joyful, foolhardy tribe of unshakeable will. Men built like the karate champion from the Demo, with tattooed torsos and copper-colored skin smoothed by sea-spray caresses, wearing brown leather loincloths, their muscles twitching, eager to exterminate the vermin. As long as this tribe remained alive, my little brother was not entirely lost.

But one morning I understood that the tribe had sustained a defeat.

Sam kept a chinchilla in his room: Helmut. A fat ball of gray fur that led a peaceful rodent's existence in a large plastic cage. Wood shavings, a water bottle, a wheel, and a little hay; the usual stuff. My mother had brought it back from a pet store one day, referring to that kind of a place as "hell on earth," where animals lived in "absolutely ghastly" conditions.

That morning—it was a few days before the return to school—I was in my room unpacking the brand new school supplies I'd just gone and bought with my mother. I always liked preparing to go back to school: the smell of new exercise books, pencils, erasers, and dividers; ticking off the list as you go; the things you own for the first time (that year, I made the happy discovery of a pair of compasses). I liked everything to do with beginnings, that moment when you imagine that things will occur according to a predefined plan, that each new element will reach you on a conveyor belt like a package in a sorting center and all you have to do is put it away in the right place. Headings in blue, subheadings in red. One eraser for the pencil, another kind for the fountain pen. Snacks in the front pocket of the schoolbag, water bottle in the side pouch. The math binder, with one divider for fractions, another for geometry, a third for multiplication tables, and the last for exercises. A few hours of warmth and tenderness like a mother's belly, during which I could entertain the illusion of possessing a semblance of control over the course of my

existence; as if there were a rampart pro-
tecting me from the hyena. Obviously I
always ended up realizing that there were
unclassifiable pages which were neither
really exercises, nor really geometry, nor
really multiplications. That life was a big
soup in a mixer where you had to try and
avoid being shredded by the blades.

I was busy packing my felt-tips into my
pencil case when I heard a strange noise
from Sam's room. A squealing. I tiptoed to
his door, which was ajar, and found Sam
kneeling on the floor holding Helmut down
with one hand while pressing a thumbtack
into his paw with the other. The chinchilla
writhed in pain while emitting shrill cries
of distress.

"What are you doing?"
He looked at me with big, empty eyes.
There was not the slightest trace of guilt in
them. I saw merely that I had interrupted a
game. And it had been so long since he'd
last enjoyed himself that for a fraction of a
second I felt bad about spoiling what
seemed to be a pleasurable moment. I closed
the door. I didn't say anything to anyone. I
think I persuaded myself that a chinchilla's

nervous system must be quite a basic thing, and that it was therefore worth the sacrifice if it helped my brother smile again until we reached August 29. Not to mention that, taking the cycle of reincarnation into consideration, this was excellent for Helmut's karma. Indeed, Helmut died a few weeks later. Heart attack.

AUGUST 29 FINALLY came. I woke early. From my window, I could see Little Gallows Wood floating in a pink mist. I thought that Monica must have wanted to robe this day in a magical light.

Monica had asked me to bring her the valuable object in the morning so that she would have all day to bewitch it. I had assessed the matter from all angles and had concluded that the most powerful object in the house, the only one that had true sentimental value, was the elephant tusk. Nothing meant more to my father. If the house were on fire, I think he would have saved his trophy first, before Sam and me. I needed to get the elephant tusk all the way over to Monica's in the morning without my father entering the carcass room throughout the entire day. The only weakness in the plan was that, being a Saturday, he didn't have to go to work. If he noticed it was missing, I didn't want to imagine what he would be capable of.

The house was asleep. The Demo was asleep. Even the goats were still asleep in their pen. I had to wait until everyone was awake to get up. It all had to appear as normal as possible. The first to wake was always my mother. She would immediately go say good morning to Coco (who would greet her with the usual singing exercises) before stepping outside to feed the goats. That was the signal Sam and I would wait for to get up ourselves.

I lay there for a long while staring at the ceiling. I thought about the vermin in Sam's head. I thought about the hyena. By that evening, the battle would be won, and all of this would never have existed. This was the last day of my draft life. My father would still fly into his rages, of course, and my mother would still be an amoeba. But I was going to get my little brother back. As well as his laughter with all the baby teeth showing.

Coco screeched. I got up. My clothes were

waiting on a chair: I had prepared them the previous evening. I went downstairs to have my breakfast. My father was still sleeping. I speedily shoveled down a bowl of cereal. Sam had joined me without a word and was drinking a glass of milk in little sips, seemingly elsewhere. I couldn't stop myself from telling him, "It'll all work out, just wait and see." He frowned, above his milk mustache.

"What are you talking about?"

"Nothing, you'll see."

The carcass room was right next to that of my parents. It was risky going to fetch the elephant tusk with my father sleeping just a few yards away. But it was even riskier to wait until he was up. I silently made my way up to the landing. I knew exactly which floorboards to avoid so it wouldn't squeak. I entered and closed the door behind me. The hyena gnawed me with her gaze, as she always did. I felt as if my father was staring at me through her.

The elephant tusk hung on two hooks. I lifted it. Its weight surprised me, it was much heavier than I had imagined. I was just wrapping it in a bath towel when I heard a noise from my father's room. He was getting up. I stopped breathing. His giant mass shook a floorboard that ran beneath my feet. He came out of the bedroom, his profile in the dawn light casting a shadow under the door. The shadow didn't move for a few seconds. My gaze was riveted to the door handle. He sniffed, cleared his throat, then went off to the bathroom. I waited for the noise of the shower before daring to move, then I went downstairs, the tusk under my arm, wrapped in the towel. My mother was in the kitchen and I exited the house without being seen.

I ran as fast as I could toward the wood and Monica's house, and knocked at her door. When she opened it, she seemed like she was still not quite awake. I found her even more beautiful than usual. She smiled from behind her long gray mussy hair.

"Hey kid! Want to come in?"

I stepped inside and unwrapped the piece of ivory. Her eyes grew wide.

"But, what is that?"

"This is the most precious object in my house. My father hunted it; he's really attached to it."

"And he's OK with us using it?"

"No, he's not! But he won't notice, since we're going back in time."

"Clever, that."

She pondered for a few seconds, her hand on the ivory. "But, you know, I don't need such a powerful object. I was thinking more of a teddy bear or something."

She thought a little longer.

"You must take this tusk back where you found it, then bring me a soft toy, OK?"

"No, that's much too dangerous. My father's already up. I can't return home now with this. If he catches me, he'll …"

My mouth got all twisted, words sticking in my throat, and two fat tears fell. I hated that. I didn't like crying anyway, but when it took me by surprise, I got so angry with myself.

"I can't take this thing back. We have to travel back in time, it's the only solution."

Monica looked at my tears as if they were her own. Her eyes flicked back and forth. It called to mind a word I'd learned at school: *disconcerted*. She was disconcerted.

"But … You know that this is all just a game?"

Her words hit me like a slap in the face.

My brain discerned everything that was monstrous in that phrase before I had even fully deciphered its meaning. A game? It was anything but. I made a superhuman effort to control my tears and my anger.

"The car is ready, I've cobbled everything together like it should be, I just need a storm. And you told me you could make the storm. It's going to work! Tonight we go back and we save my little brother. You told me so! We save my little brother, we save the ice-cream man, and the images will stop eating away at my brain. You told me so!"

That's when her own tears started. She took my face in her hands and shook her head.

"I'm sorry."

"But you're a fairy ..."

She shook her head again.

I needed to run, just run, and flee that phrase: "But ... You know that this is all just a game?"

* * *

I left the house, ran out of the claw mark, and reached the cornfield. I ran so fast, I felt as though my legs were having difficulty keeping up. The sharp leaves slashed my cheeks, but I didn't care. If they'd been capable of slicing me to pieces, of making me vanish into slivers of flesh to fall over the cornfield like a red rain, I would have been grateful to them. I reached the top of the sandy slope and jumped. There, too, I would have wished to smash into the bottom, for it all to be over, to hear the hyena's laugh one last time, then silence. And darkness. But I simply landed a few yards down, in the yellow sand. I sobbed there for a few minutes, my fingers digging into the sand, clawing at the wet ground hard enough to break my nails. The low morning sun came to lick away my tears, and a warm breeze, as light as a shadow, caressed my hair. They both seemed to want to soothe me. It didn't work. A burning rage had permeated me as thoroughly as if it had been poured down my throat. I ran to the car for traveling back in time, grabbed a metal bar, and began hitting it. I hit the windshield, I hit the hood, I hit the microwave, I hit that whole year of work, plans, research, and hope.

"What's all this?" It was the owner. I

looked him straight in the eye, holding my iron bar. I thought I should hit him too. He had to pay, someone had to pay, no matter who. The thing shredding my insides needed to burst out and eat someone. I leapt. The owner grabbed the bar with one hand and struck me in the face with the other, sending me flying against a car. It was such a violent impact that I couldn't breathe for a few seconds. He looked at me, flushed, the veins standing out on his neck. He still held the iron bar in his hand. He came closer, raised the bar above his head and yelled:

"Get out of my yard, filthy brat!"

I got up and ran toward the sandy slope, the roots, the cornfield, the little wood, and my house. For the first time in my life my house seemed like a refuge, and I wasn't sure that was good news. I snuck in through the front door so I wouldn't be seen. Sam was playing silently in his room. I lay down on my bed and waited for the fires in my belly to die down. Then I started to think. My most urgent problem was the elephant tusk. I needed to fetch it from Monica's and put it back in its place without my father noticing. I got up. The idea of returning to Monica's gave me a weird feeling. Something between longing and disgust.

I took Dovka with me as I went downstairs. Most of the time my parents didn't ask about my comings and goings, but as a precaution I preferred to have the excuse of walking the dog. Outside on the terrace, my father was drinking his coffee and watching my mother give the goats some hay. She was singing to them. She said it did them good, particularly Cumin, who, according to her, had a neurotic temperament. He was a nasty animal, for sure, vicious and aggressive. But it wasn't his fault; like Coco, he couldn't stand being caged. What's more, that pen was too small for five goats. But my mother refused to part with a single one of them. So she sang them songs. And my father watched her, although the singing didn't seem to soothe *him* at all. Quite the opposite. He was pulling that face, his mouth twisting, the right side drooping like a child about to cry, the left upper lip rising like that of a growling dog, and he made weird movements with his jaw.

I stepped into the garden. "Where you

going?" my father's voice barked out behind me. I flinched.

"To walk Dovka."

"Got a sweetheart, is that it?" He gave a dry laugh.

"No, no."

"You think I didn't notice that secretive face of yours. You've got a sweetheart!" He laughed again.

"No really, I ..."

I scurried off. He knew I was hiding something. He didn't know what, but he had sensed it. The fear caused me to start crying again.

That's how I arrived at Monica's, with my cheeks burning and wet. I didn't care what on earth she might think. I just wanted to collect that tusk as quickly as possible. She was waiting for me outside on the tree trunk. The tusk lay beside her wrapped in the towel. I took it and muttered, "I've got to put it back." Monica grasped my wrist: "Wait, kid." Her voice was hoarse. And she, too, had red cheeks.

"I was fibbing about the storm, but not about the rest. Not about Marie Curie. You've got gumption, chicklet. The gumption of those who achieve great things. You took a real smack in the head today, but … you must carry on fighting. I'm sorry I'm no fairy godmother. But you're not just anybody, lady. And if anyone tells you different, you just tell them from me they can go fuck themselves."

I didn't feel like listening to her, I just wanted that tusk to be back in place on the wall it should never have left. She grasped my wrist tighter.

"Will you come back and see me?"

I nodded, knowing full well that I wouldn't. I just wanted her to let go. I set off back to the Demo. From the little wood, I could see our house and our garden. The vegetation allowed me to observe without being seen. My mother was still singing in the goat pen, but my father was no longer on the terrace. I couldn't take the risk of entering the house with the tusk if I didn't know where he was. I walked round to the street. The little path leading to the front door was lined with box trees, and I was able to hide my package at the foot of one. I tiptoed to the door. The sound of the TV told me that my father was exactly where I hoped, on his couch. I went back to get the tusk.

When I stepped inside, Coco greeted me with her cry. I closed the door as quietly as I could. It was cool in the hallway compared with the heat outdoors. The skin on my legs quivered. As I snuck toward the stairs, I had a sense of being pursued by the hyena. I could almost feel her hot breath on the small of my back. A ball of incandescent dread had burned into my chest and I could hardly breathe. I was nearly at the top of the stairs.

"Well then?"

I wilted, and turned to look at my father, who was scrutinizing me from the living-room doorway. My body turned into a large pool of blood that cascaded down the stairs. All that was left of me were two bare eyeballs lying on the wooden floor watching him. I understood what my mother must have felt when his rages escalated. I understood what it was to be an amoeba. Yet I would have preferred to be an amoeba a thousand times over rather than suffer the fate he had in store for me. I couldn't enunciate a sound. Pools of blood don't speak.

"Was he pleased to see you, your sweetheart? Hahahahaha!"

His laugh was like a python coiling itself around me before tightening in suffocation. I was obliged to nod.

"What's that you got there?"

He jerked his chin at the towel.

"... Stuff ... that I collected in the woods to make something with."

His left eye narrowed, his lips curled. He looked at me the way he looked at my mother when she sang to her goats. Then his gaze fixed on the towel. He made to step forward. The parakeets screeched in the garden and Coco answered them. I could no longer see my future. I usually had quite a precise vision of my short-term future: what I was going to do with my day, my week; what I was going to eat and read. Now it was all blank. My father was going to discover the tusk and everything would slip out of control, without me having any idea what the consequences would be.

The sound of the intro to the lunchtime news echoed from the living room. My father froze. His head swiveled back and forth several times from the TV to the towel. Then he turned and went back to sit on his bear pelt.

I had learned from my reading that the fear hormone was called adrenaline. I must have been having an adrenaline overdose because I could hardly see a thing. A black fog pierced with a few points of phosphorescence had filled my head. I used my sensory memory to get to the first floor and reach the carcass room, like when I walked through the dark to go pee at night. I entered. Sam was there, by the hyena. I unwrapped the tusk and placed it back on its hooks. He watched me do so with his little expressionless face. I didn't feel like explaining things to him. Too long, too complicated.

That evening I waited for him to come lie in my bed, as usual. He didn't. Nor the following nights. We never slept together again.

* * *

That summer finished as it began. A long drawn-out death. I waited for it to end, knowing full well that this end would offer me no solace. It took me a few weeks to comprehend what Monica had said to me, "You took a real smack in the head today, but you must carry on fighting." What if I had only gotten the method wrong? What if I had only lost a battle? What if my struggle was only just beginning? A struggle that would last for years.

Ultimately, it really didn't matter, the aim was to travel back in time. So time was not important. In fact, nothing was important. But I simply couldn't accept spending the rest of my life watching the vermin eat my little brother's brain, and losing him forever. I would change that, even if I had to devote my entire existence to it. Or I would die. There was no other way.

Science then. Only science. I was done with magic. It was a childish thing. And I was no longer a child.

The school year began.

On September 26, Sam turned eight. My father bought him a subscription to the shooting range.

I ENTERED MIDDLE school that year. Everything was different. The boys began to chase the girls and the girls played at being women. This whole little world was in effervescence, completely absorbed in the great hormonal muddle. Each person sported the proof of their admission to puberty like a trophy. An embryonic mustache here, a burgeoning bust there. I felt a little alien to this hysterical fauna, particularly when their herd instinct made them aggressive. There was this girl in my class whom the others made fun of all the time, I don't know why. There was no particular reason for it. I think they just needed to purge their excess emotion, and so it fell on her.

My own passion was for the science classes, particularly physics. I wanted to understand the workings of the laws of temporality, the principle of causality, the metapsychological paradox, and the space-time curve. According to the causality principle, the effect cannot precede the cause; which would therefore make time travel impossible, although some scientists refuted this theory and spoke of "retro-causality." If there existed the slightest possibility of going back in time, I had to find and exploit it, in order to see Sam laugh again, with his baby teeth, and his big green eyes.

My teachers were delighted by my curiosity and what they called my "keen-mindedness." In truth it was just a question of motivation. If only they knew that a little boy's laughter depended on it, but I couldn't tell them that.

The following summer arrived and, with the start of vacation, the cat disappearances began. Neighborhood cats. There were notices all over the Demo. Distraught boys and girls with big tearful eyes called at every door, brandishing photos of their four-legged companions, pursuing their investigations for days, as Sam and I had done when Dovka disappeared. I never said anything, but I knew. Sam had become a serial killer: Jack the Ripper of the Demo's cats.

I got proof of this one evening while taking Dovka out for a walk. Sam wasn't there. He had gone to the shooting range with my father. A new relationship had developed between them, and this had become their Saturday-afternoon ritual. It seemed as though Sam had become worthy of our father's attention as soon as he was capable of holding a gun. They started having conversations, of which I understood nothing, about Smith & Wesson, Beretta, Pierre Artisan, and Browning. This or that caliber for this or that animal. How to pierce a rhinoceros's hide. How to destroy a vital organ at several hundred yards. But my brother couldn't yet join a hunting party, he had to learn to shoot at fixed targets first.

Sam's features continued to change. He no longer looked like a little boy. He was eight years old and his internal chemistry had mutated. I was sure it was the vermin still polluting him. Even his smell was no longer the same. It was as if his scent had gone bad. He gave off something troubling; it was subtle but I sensed it. It was in his smile, what I called his *new* smile. A grimace that said: "Take another step toward me and I'll bite your head off." My brother's grin stank. But I kept his secret.

That day, I was looking for an old cassette tape on which I'd recorded a compilation of The Cranberries. Not finding it anywhere in my room, I went to check in Sam's. It was hidden in a drawer in his desk. I put it in my Walkman and went out with Dovka. I walked her every day. I liked wandering through the fields and the woods. And she liked chasing rabbits. It was the terrier in her.

I loved the perfect indifference of nature. Whatever was going on with me, nature pursued its precise plan for survival and reproduction. My father would knock my mother around and the birds didn't give a damn. I found that comforting. They continued chirping, the trees creaked, and the wind sang through the leaves of the sweet chestnut. I was nothing to them. Merely a spectator. And this show never stopped. The set changed according to the season, but every year it was the same summer, with its light and its scent; and every year the blackberries fruited on the brambles that grew along the track.

I often came across Feather Girl out with her little boy, Takeshi, in his stroller. So we walked a little way together. She always smelled of modeling clay. I eventually figured out her routine and I adapted my own accordingly to increase my chances of meeting her while out walking. She talked a lot and I liked the sound of her voice. She spoke with a touch of an accent that I associated with somewhere down south.

Those moments spent with Feather Girl had become vital to me, even though I wasn't quite aware of the fact. She told me that she worked as an educator in a local high school where her karate champion was the Phys. Ed. teacher.

"He really was a champion, you know. A few years ago he was even selected for the World Championships in Sydney. But the day before leaving he slipped while stepping out of the shower, and broke his coccyx. That was the end of his career. He's never really recovered."

So I went out with Dovka that day and I walked through the Demo hoping to see

Feather Girl. The sunnier it was, the grayer seemed the facades. The light somehow brought out the full extent of their ugliness. It was like a brutal realization that, even under optimal conditions, this place would always be desperately hideous. I passed a minuscule garden in which a very fat man was sleeping in swimming trunks on a dirty plastic sun lounger. His skin was white underneath, red on top. It made me think of raspberry panna cotta. A bit further on, another man, also very fat, was washing his car, stripped to the waist. I recalled the karate champion's torso and I wondered how it was possible for two such different torsos to exist in the same animal species. I was starting to reason like a scientist, by dint of studying.

I came across a little girl who must have been Sam's age, perhaps a bit younger. On a traffic light she had stuck a notice with a photo of a cat. I lowered my gaze and hurried on. I was nearly at Feather Girl's house. She was just coming out with the stroller. Perfect timing. When I reached her, she smiled at me. We left the Demo and headed toward the fields. Takeshi quickly fell asleep. I thought to myself that falling asleep while being walked in a stroller in the sun must be one of life's greatest pleasures. Feather Girl flicked her hair back with a light shake of her head. "I'm pregnant," she said. "With a little girl." Something in her voice turned my heart into a snow globe. She shook it and thousands of glittering particles whirled inside of me. This baby was not yet born and it had already generated more love in its mother than I had been able to produce in both my parents combined over twelve years of existence. Far from drawing any bitterness from this, I saw in it a kind of consolation, and security. At that moment I realized that I loved Feather Girl.

We strolled and chatted for around an hour, before heading back to the Demo. She went home, while Dovka and I returned to our house the way we came. The guy was still sleeping on his sun lounger, but facedown this time. He was red all over now. I thought of a malignant melanoma.

I remembered that I had brought my Walkman, so I put on my headphones and pressed *Play*. What I heard was gut-wrenching. It wasn't the voice of Dolores O'Riordan of The Cranberries. It was screams. Screams of tortured cats. I recognized the distress that I'd heard in Helmut's squeals. I ripped off the headphones, on the verge of puking. I had already noticed that Sam listened to his Walkman every time the ice-cream man's truck passed. I knew he did that so as not to hear the "Flower Waltz," but I thought it was music he was listening to.

I didn't know what I should do with the tape. My first thought was to destroy it to prevent the vermin in his head from feeding on those screams. I remembered that terrifying scene in *Jurassic Park* where a cow is lowered into the velociraptor enclosure on a steel hoist. You see only the vegetation move. After a few seconds, the harness is winched back up, empty and disjointed. The vermin in my brother's head were as vicious and voracious as the velociraptors in *Jurassic Park*. On the other hand, I was scared that, not being able to find his tape, he would decide to record another. My silence had already made me sufficiently complicit, I didn't want more martyred animals on my conscience. When I got home, I had just enough time to put it back in its place before he returned from the shooting range.

* * *

The closer my father and brother became, the more isolated I felt. My relationship with Sam remained screwed unless I managed to change the past. And I knew that I couldn't hope for greater closeness with my father, because I was a girl. Even if I had wanted to get into guns and hunting, they wouldn't have let me in their club. Sometimes I tried to join their discussions, but I was systematically rebuffed by a "You wouldn't understand." It didn't incense me. I accepted as self-evident that a boy was worth more than a girl and that there were areas closed off to me. It was normal, it was just how it was, it was probably genetic. And it's true that I had difficulty imagining Marie Curie handling an AK-47. My father had an heir and it could only be a boy. I knew that the sole reason he had conceived a second child with my mother was to have a son. If Sam had been a girl, my mother would have had to endure a third pregnancy.

What struck me was that my father had only begun to show an interest in Sam when the hyena had ensconced herself in his head. I think that he loved the vermin and did all he could to feed them. But there was also the fact that my body had changed a lot that year. Everything was fuller. My breasts, of course, but also my thighs, my hips, and my behind. I didn't know what to do with it all. I didn't pay much attention to it, but I noticed that people started to look at me differently as my shape changed. Particularly my father. I had turned from being an insignificant little thing to a repulsive little thing. I had the impression of having done something bad. Sometimes I caught Sam eyeing the shape of my breasts beneath my T-shirt almost reproachfully. I felt like I'd turned into some disgusting creature. I withdrew more and more from him, becoming increasingly alone.

Logic would have had it that I should grow closer to my mother, but what sort of relationship can you have with an amoeba?

I tried, but her conversation was limited to basics: "Finish your mash potato," or "You need new shoes," or "This sun will be good for Nutmeg's psoriasis," or "Animals are kinder than humans." For all that, I still liked giving her a hand in the garden now and then. An afternoon spent pulling up weeds in silence gave me the impression of sharing some sort of bond.

EVERY YEAR, THERE was a yard sale and street fair in the Demo, the last weekend of August. A bunch of carnies took over the streets, setting up stalls from which emanated the smells of fat and sugar. There was cotton candy, rubber-duck fishing, a shooting gallery, and bumper cars. The inhabitants placed unwanted items from their lofts in front of their houses. They came out and greeted each other, which made me believe that something was in the process of changing, that people were really getting to know each other and forge connections that might vaguely resemble friendship or love. But no sooner had the carnies left than everyone returned to their solitary torpor in front of the TV, cultivating their pick of depression, bitterness, misanthropy, apathy, or diabetes.

My mother, brother, and I went along each year. I loved the *smoutebollen*—doughnuts dusted with confectioners' sugar—despite the fact that ever since what happened to the old ice-cream man, I felt a certain apprehension toward these people who worked behind huge vats of boiling oil. I always wanted twelve smoutebollen. My mother told me each time that I would be perfectly content with eight, but I stuck to my guns: twelve was what I wanted. So each time she bought me twelve. And each time I ate six.

The previous year, my brother had triumphed at the shooting gallery. He picked up the air rifle, inserted the lead pellets, and hit the target while barely looking at it. It was as if he wasn't especially interested in plugging holes in an inanimate object. This year, it didn't attract him at all. He had the shooting range, with real guns. For the first time ever, he refused to come with my mother and me.

As we walked past the rubber-duck fishing stall, my mother shot a dirty look at the carnie handing out goldfish in plastic bags to the children. This was the reason I'd never been able to have a go: it was out of the question to give this animal torturer a penny. A little further on I saw Feather Girl. She was selling Takeshi's baby clothes while he played with his Playmobil on the sidewalk next to her. His belly had already grown rounder since early summer. I was just walking over to say hello when a voice stopped me in my tracks.

"Hey, it's Dovka!"

I turned around. The karate champion knelt there, busily stroking my doggie who couldn't get enough of him. Was it possible that she remembered? The Champion laid his gaze upon me. His wild-horse of a body stood up. The warm thing I'd felt swelling in my belly the year before had matured. This time, as well as the spreading warmth, there was a scent of brown sugar, and a feeling of moist softness I wanted to snuggle into.

I felt—without understanding why— that I was betraying my little brother by permitting my belly to produce this heat. Then again, I instinctively knew that what was going on there, in the depths of my guts, was feeding a beast capable of confronting the hyena. A powerful and blood-thirsty beast devoted to my pleasure only. The Champion came closer. He looked at me differently too. He detected the warmth in my belly, I sensed it. But it didn't appear to disgust him. The shorts I was wearing suddenly seemed too short. I felt naked in the middle of this crowd. He smiled at me. I recalled the expression on his face as he slammed his fist into the head of the drunk on his moldy old couch. That hideous expression of a perverse monster excited by the smell of blood was so far removed from this face of a civilized man that I suddenly wondered if the incident had really taken place.

"She's properly grown up, your little doggie."

"Yes."

"But she's still got something of the puppy about her, it's cute."

"Mom, this is the man who helped me get Dovka back when she was taken."

"Really? That's so kind ..."

She didn't have the slightest idea what I was talking about. Her gaze was fixed on some vague point in the distance, but I knew she wasn't looking at anything special. Her brain was just in standby mode. I told myself that all those blows she'd received from my father must have affected her mental faculties.

The Champion looked at me for a few seconds. I still felt naked. Then Feather Girl called to him, and we each went our own way. I didn't feel like any smoutebollen that day. My mother bought a few gypsophila seedlings for the garden and we went home.

That's how summer ended. The cats continued disappearing, and when there were no more cats, the notices stuck to lampposts were replaced with those seeking missing dogs. I made Dovka sleep in my room from then on. Sam was becoming a stranger to me. But I was sure that my little brother still existed somewhere, deep inside. Occasionally, fleetingly, I saw a glow on his face, the hint of a smile, a gleam in his eyes, and I knew that all was not lost. So I clung to the certainty of going back in time and altering the course of our lives.

I was happy to return to school and continue my studies.

* * *

At the end of the school year, my science teacher called my parents in. My mother came alone. My teacher insisted that I be present during the meeting. I didn't like him much because he smelled of sour cream. And also because he drew connections between scientific and philosophical concepts, which were interesting but slowed down the class. And his classes were already much too slow, particularly math class. I got bored. The other pupils were preoccupied with their crushes and their skin problems, so this rhythm suited them. They had never heard the hyena's laugh. If they had, they would have understood the futility of their preoccupations. Me? I wanted to progress. I was thirteen and we were still being taught about cell composition. I also didn't like my teacher because he was useless, through and through—his smell betrayed as much. He had simply given up. Indeed, everyone at the school was useless. The teachers, the pupils. The former were idiotically old and the latter would become so. A bit of acne, a little sexual intercourse, some further education, kids, work, and presto! They'll be old and will have served no purpose. Whereas I wanted to be Marie Curie. I had no time to lose.

But that day, my science teacher seemed to have decided to serve a purpose. He sat us down in his classroom, my mother and me. There wafted the vague odor of raw onion beneath the bluish tinge of the fluorescents. He addressed my mother.

"So, we discussed your daughter at our teachers' meeting. She has exceptional abilities in math and the sciences."

He looked at me.

"We've never seen that. I don't know where she gets this passion from, but that's really what it is: a passion. She knew the whole of this year's program by the end of September. So we'd like it if she moved up to the next class when school starts again."

My mother had the look of a cow to which someone has just explained Heisenberg's uncertainty principle.

"Ah, that's good."

At which point he addressed me directly, a piece of paper in his hand.

"I have a friend who lives close to you.

Usually, I send him those of my pupils who are lagging behind, for some remedial classes. But I think you should go see him, you'll have much to talk about, the pair of you. He used to teach quantum physics at Tel Aviv University. You must meet him."

He took my hand, placed the scrap of paper in my palm, closed my fingers over it, and repeated, "You must meet him." I was surprised at his insistence. This was the first time I'd really seen him concerned with anything. My mother thanked him and we went home, where I helped my mother prepare the meal. I had noticed that when my father started to become edgy, she served red meat, as if she hoped that the bloody flesh would calm his rage. But I knew that blood wouldn't calm him. He had to penetrate living flesh, be it with his fist or a .22 caliber bullet.

I remembered the episode of the steak and the smashed plate. My mother too. The scar she bore beneath her eye reminded her of it each day, and she had not dared cook red meat properly since then. She vaguely seared it, but inside it was raw and cold. That evening she prepared a leg of lamb.

When we sat down to eat, my father asked her why we had been called in to school.

"Because she has good grades in math. They want to move her up a class."

"I don't have good grades, I have the *top* grade. And it's in math *and* the sciences."

"Ass-licker." This from Sam.

I tried to ignore his attacks, which were becoming more and more frequent. I sensed it had something to do with my changing body. But I also knew it wasn't my little brother talking, it was that filth in his head. Which only strengthened my determination.

My father gave a hollow laugh. Then, in his deep voice, the one that preceded his attacks, he commented, "That's just great. We've got us an Einstein in the family." His jaw made that weird movement. The one that conveyed his desire to lash out. We continued eating the raw lamb in silence. But I understood that, from now on, just like my mother, I, too, had become a prey.

ON THE SCRAP of paper my teacher gave me, there was a name and an address: Professor Yotam Pavlović, 11 Avenue du Baleau. It was in the Demo, on the opposite corner to that of our house. I went there the next day. I brought Dovka with me because Sam was at home and I didn't want to leave her alone with him. On the way, I passed the house of Feather Girl and the Champion. I hadn't seen her for a few months. I told myself she must have given birth to her little girl.

A cloud of green parakeets flew across the sky, as I walked up the street to number 11. It was a gray and black house, like all the others, but with a well-kept garden. There were window boxes planted with geraniums. I rang the bell. A man opened the door. He was of average height, with white hair and thick black eyebrows above an unsettling gaze. He had a plaited goatee with a little green bead at the end.

"Yes?"

I explained the reason for my visit. He invited me in. The hallway was completely dark.

"Ya," he called out, "put your mask on, we have a visitor."

I didn't see the person he was speaking to, but I glimpsed movement. The sound of a radio came from the small living room to my right. Classical music. I followed the professor into the dining room. There was a heavy table of dark oak, a bouquet of red roses on a sideboard that matched the table, and, on the wall, a huge, shiny whiteboard covered in diagrams and formulas in black marker.

The professor gestured to a chair and I sat down. He observed me for a few seconds from under his thick eyebrows. I observed him too. There was something strange about this man. A mixture of self-confidence and shyness. But no trace of violence. He rolled the bead of his goatee between his fingers.

"Why are you interested in physics?"

"I don't know. I just like it."

"No, you *do* know."

I didn't lower my gaze.

"But it's none of my business, right?"

He had a funny way of pronouncing words, which I'd never heard before. I liked it.

"What can you tell me about wave-particle duality?"

"Err … that they are two separate notions in classical mechanics. But in quantum physics they are said to be two facets of the same phenomenon."

"Which phenomenon?"

"Well, light. It can behave like a collection of particles—photons—or like a wave. It depends on the experimental context."

"Where did you read about that? It's not part of the school curriculum."

"*The Quantum World* by Stéphane Deligeorges."

He observed me for a few seconds more. I wondered if I should be wary of him or not. I glimpsed a lacerated soul who, like my father, deciphered my thoughts with terrifying ease.

"You can come see me once a week, I'll help you progress. Can you give me your phone number? I'd like to speak to your parents."

He held out a pen and a notepad.

"Why do you want to speak to my parents?"

"Because I'll need their agreement. And I have to talk to them about money too; it won't be free."

"My mother will give you her agreement. But they won't pay. I'll sort that out myself."

I wrote my number down on the notepad.

"But call during the day. I'd prefer you speak to my mother rather than my father."

I had a strong sense that it was better my father not be reminded that I liked the sciences. What I'd seen in his reaction the previous day suggested that I was treading on dangerous ground. His taste for annihilation was forcing me to develop myself in silence. On tiptoe.

The professor saw me to the front door. The person in the small living room hadn't moved, judging by the sound from the radio. I cast a furtive glance, but I couldn't see anyone from where I was. The professor waved me goodbye. We had agreed I would return the following week.

I needed to earn some money. This professor was the only person I knew with whom I could discuss wave-particle duality, the Aharonov-Bohm effect, or the Stern-Gerlach experiment. These were notions familiar to me, that I had read about in books but which I didn't understand fully yet. I decided to hire myself out as a babysitter. I could start with Feather Girl. What with her two children, she would certainly need a hand. I went round to hers. She was happy to see me. The Champion wasn't there, and I felt a prick of disappointment in my throat. Feather Girl introduced me to her little girl, Yumi. Takeshi had grown a lot. I talked to her about my babysitting idea, and she said yes straightaway. "Because of the children, the two of us don't get much time together." She suggested one evening the following week, the night before my appointment with Professor Pavlović, which was perfect. I asked if I could come with Dovka. "I can't leave her home alone." She was a bit surprised at this, but agreed.

It just remained to convince my father. The lessons with Professor Pavlović would take place during the day, while he was at the amusement park, but I wasn't going to be able to hide the babysitting from him. I looked for a pretext to have to earn money, something that would please him. I was beginning to understand that the slightest sign of volition on my part risked stirring his animosity. He expected me to become like my mother. An empty envelope, devoid of desire. He didn't know who his daughter really was. But at thirteen years old I remained at his mercy. I would therefore have to deceive him until I was old enough to go live far away.

It was two days later. Sam and my mother had gone out, so I seized the opportunity. My father was sitting on the terrace cleaning his guns. This was how he spent his Sunday afternoons, when he wasn't at the shooting range or off hunting. His guns were the only things in the house my mother didn't have to clean. Even the stuffed animals, she had to brush regularly to remove the dust. I was happy he was doing it out on the terrace because the products he used smelled strongly and, when he did it inside, it stank up the house for days.

"Dad?"

"Mmmmm."

"I ... I was thinking that this year, for Sam's birthday, I would like to give him a present. He'll be turning ten, it's an important one ..."

He was scrubbing the barrel of his rifle with a special little brush.

"Yes. And?"

"And I need money for that. I'm old enough to go earn it now. I could do some babysitting ..."

He put his gun down and looked at me the way he had the day I'd stolen the elephant tusk. He sensed that I was lying. I lowered my gaze, telling myself that it wasn't really a lie. I was doing all this for Sam. I tried to imitate how my mother behaved, to appear as transparent as possible. "ok," he said, then picked up his rifle and continued scrubbing it. I stuck up notices offering my babysitting services all over the Demo.

The night agreed with Feather Girl came around. She opened the door. The Champion wasn't there, he would be meeting her at a restaurant. Their living room hadn't really changed since I'd seen it the first time, the day Dovka was taken. There was just a bit more mess. Takeshi was sitting on the couch watching *The Lion King*. He gave little cries of joy when he saw Dovka. Yumi was burbling in her playpen.

Feather Girl left me a list of instructions. "Takeshi sometimes has pain in his legs, because he's growing." So she showed me a bottle of massage oil, just in case. Then she left to go meet the Champion, having hugged and kissed all three of us as if I were also one of her children.

I sat down near Takeshi and watched Simba talking to the ghost of his father in the clouds. That's when I realized that Disney must have been largely inspired by *Hamlet* while developing the script: the specter of the father who talks to his son ("Remember who you are"); the king's brother who kills him to seize the throne; the exiled hero; the omnipresent image of the skull; the reference to madness, embodied by the monkey. The only difference was that Horatio had become a flatulent warthog.

When the cartoon had finished, Takeshi

grumbled a bit about going to bed, but I managed after two songs and two stories. Yumi fell asleep in my arms while drinking her bottle. I placed her in her cot without her waking up. A little later in the evening, Takeshi had some pain in his legs, so I massaged them with the oil. I watched his big black eyes close, his mouth slacken, and his little body fall into a deep sleep. I lost myself in contemplation of this perfect spectacle for a few minutes, and I wondered whether this kid would ever realize the unbelievable luck he had. To be born here. To be the son of Feather Girl and the Champion. To be loved with so much love.

I returned to the living room and spent the rest of the evening watching whatever was on TV. If I had a bottle of Glenfiddich, I thought, I would be the worthy daughter of my father. I was starting to nod off when Feather Girl came home. The Champion was waiting in his car to take me home. She gave me my pay and kissed me goodbye. I got into the Champion's Golf. "I could have walked home," I said, "it's just down the road." He smiled at me: "You never know."

The swelling warmth in my belly rose

into my throat, making me take short, spasmodic breaths. I sat there in the car, my body a few inches from his. When he placed his hand on the gear lever, it brushed against my knee. The warmth in my belly sank between my legs. Something began to throb down there. I think that if the Champion had touched me then, I would have fainted. What he had done to the drunk that time scared me—I felt a kind of fear bordering on disgust—and yet, that warm feeling ... "Did it all go OK?" he asked.

"Yes," I said.

Less than fifteen seconds was all it took to cover the two hundred yards from his house to mine. It was totally absurd, this car journey. He parked his Golf on the roadside by our garden hedge. I didn't feel like leaving him. The Champion's existence suddenly seemed essential to my survival. I would have liked to have asked him to keep me close to him, forever. I would have said nothing, demanded nothing, just the warmth of his presence, his body close to mine, and this thing that throbbed between my legs. But he said, "Thanks a lot. See you soon!" And I replied, "Thank you.

See you soon!" And home I went.

I went to bed imagining what would have happened if he had placed his lips on mine. And his hands on my body. I knew I wasn't allowed to think like this, that it was a bad thing. But while I was daydreaming of the Champion, my mind took off, far, far away from the hyena, and, just for a moment, I forgot that she existed.

My next session with Professor Pavlović was the following day. There was still the sound of the radio coming from the small living room. This presence intrigued me. The professor took me into the dining room. He made us some tea.

"Right, what do you want to know?"

I felt dizzy, not knowing where to start. I hadn't guessed the number of questions I had concerning quantum physics. Our session started like that, chaotically. I asked a question and the professor began to answer, drawing diagrams on his whiteboard, but I didn't give him time to finish his explanation before asking another question. I was like a starving little girl let loose in a pastry store.

At school, my hunger to learn was never

remotely satisfied: each door I wanted to open remained locked because of my teachers' ignorance. Here I had someone who opened them all to me, patiently, and let me glimpse the vastness of the territories to be explored. I knew that my delight was shared. When the professor talked about physics, it was like watching an artist on stage: he almost went into a trance, intoxicated by his passion. He taught me as much about the history of the great scientists as he did physics itself.

He was in the middle of telling me about the life of Isaac Newton when there was a movement in the dark hallway. I made out a figure coming slowly toward us. When she emerged from the darkness, I stifled a cry of terror. It was the body of an old woman dressed in blue and white checkered pajamas, but instead of a face, there was a mask: a plaster smile with lips painted red, hollow eyes, feathers, and sequins. A smooth, frozen, eternally young face, on an old woman's body.

"We have a new student, Ya."

Then, addressing me:

"This is Yael. She's my wife."

Yael nodded her head. I couldn't make out her eyes through the two dark holes. She opened a tin lying on the sideboard, took out a few cookies, and offered me one. "No thanks," I said. She turned and headed back toward the living room. Each step she took seemed to require exorbitant effort. I didn't dare ask the professor about her.

This first full session lasted three hours and I left troubled and frustrated: troubled by the encounter with Yael, and frustrated at having to wait for our next appointment—that my life wasn't one long session with Professor Pavlović.

IT DIDN'T STOP raining that summer. You'd have thought the sky was in mourning. Long wet days and long wet nights, with that endless background noise, a pattering so sad you might have wondered if nature itself was contemplating suicide. Even the hyena had stopped laughing, and Sam seemed to have lost his enthusiasm for torturing animals. But my own memory of that summer is a wonderful one, thanks to Professor Pavlović, and to several evenings spent babysitting Takeshi and Yumi. Although I babysat them no more than three or four times, those evenings had the same effect on me as a fountain in the middle of the desert. I loved those children as if they were my own younger siblings. I loved Feather Girl. And I loved the Champion. Best of all, each of those evenings ended like the first one, with those few minutes just for the two of us, the Champion and me, his hands brushing against my knees as he changed gear, my body ablaze. It was like a rollercoaster ride, a mixture of delight and apprehension, with feelings of indescribable pleasure that were terrifying in their uncontrollable power.

* * *

When the rain decided to call a truce, I loved to go walk barefoot in the goat pen.

The goats' pointed little hooves had turned the waterlogged earth into a real quagmire and I enjoyed sinking my feet in right up to the ankles. The aim of the game was to not fall over in the slippery mud. I loved the feeling of sodden earth on my bare skin, and I would play with Paprika, though our games often ended with me sliding and falling. I laughed, Dovka yapped, and the goat made joyous little leaps. Sometimes Cumin charged me and I had to throw myself out of the pen to avoid his horns. I returned home covered in mud from head to toe.

My mother tried to make me realize that at thirteen years old I should start acting like a young woman. "Men don't like slobs," she said. And this was undoubtedly true. At school, the girls no longer had play fights or chased each other. These were activities reserved for boys. They contained themselves, and struck poses. I watched them sometimes. They laughed while placing their hands in front of their mouths or sweeping strands of hair behind their ears. The gestures were subtle, graceful, like those of Feather Girl. But I knew that subtlety and grace were not part of my genetic code.

* * *

Other families called me to look after their children—word-of-mouth had been effective—and I found myself working more and more. Not only did I earn a fair amount of money, but I was able to escape meals with my family. With the income, I could afford regular visits to Professor Pavlović, where I stuffed myself with science, digesting as fast as I consumed, hungry for more.

I made rapid progress. Professor Pavlović said—laughing—that at this rate I'd have the Nobel Prize for Physics before I was twenty-five. But behind his laughter, I sensed a real fascination with this little phenomenon he was making of me.

I was frightened of Yael and her mask, but I didn't dare ask why she wore it, or why she was mute.

* * *

Late one afternoon, coming home from one of my visits to Professor Pavlović, I felt strangely uneasy as I approached the house. Was it the silence? The parakeets weren't singing; even the wind had quieted down. Or was it the attitude of Dovka, who stayed close to me, her tail down, when usually she'd be running off far ahead? I didn't know. But the hyena was on the prowl, of that I was certain. Yet I felt good that day, really good, even. I had just run into the Champion as I passed his house. He was getting out of his car. When he saw me, he smiled and waved, then came up to me, placed his hand on the small of my back, and kissed me on the cheek. That touch of his hand turned me into a human torch. His imprint remained on the skin of my lower back, radiating down to the top of my thighs in little electric jolts.

I was in precisely this state when I approached my house. And I knew that this state could last several hours, as long as the hyena didn't interfere.

My mother was doing some ironing in the living room. I went upstairs. Sam was playing with his Game Boy in the carcass room. Everything seemed normal. I went and sat down in my room, on the windowsill, to think about the Champion's body, his gaze, his hand on my back. I made acquaintance with this soft, warm creature living in my belly. I could have spent hours like that. It was a state of absence, of plenitude, of being totally in touch with my body and my senses.

That's when I heard my mother screaming from the garden. I couldn't see her because of the branches of the oak tree, but I knew she was in the goat pen. I was familiar with how she screamed when my father lost control of his anger—often aided by the Glenfiddich—but those were the frail screams of an amoeba. Nothing to compare with what ripped apart the tranquility of this late summer's day. I rushed downstairs and out to the garden. I saw my mother from behind, kneeling in the mud, leaning over something I couldn't make out. I drew closer. Cumin. The goat lay in a pool of its own fresh blood. My mother, her lips pressed to the animal's mouth, was trying in vain to revive him. In place of eyes there gaped two bloody sockets. His ears had been ripped off and now lay a few inches from their natural location. The neck had been cut so deeply that the only thing attaching the head to the body was the spinal column. And the body had been slashed in so many places, there wasn't a square inch of hide that wasn't sticky with blood. My mother desperately continued her mouth-to-mouth. I watched her for a few seconds, wondering if she would have fought with the same energy for Sam or for me. I grabbed her shoulders. "Come on, it's over." She gave a long howl, followed by sobbing. She turned, took me in her arms, and cried for a good while. A gesture of solace, but not only: I felt love too. I even thought I sensed something like: "What if something happened to you, my darling?" Perhaps I was mistaken. We remained there for several minutes, crying in each other's arms. I cried because I could hear the hyena's laugh again and I was terrified. But also because I was connecting with my mother a little, and—suddenly—I was loving her. And I cried, too, for the loss of my little brother. In getting him to slaughter Cumin, the vermin had struck hard at his bastion of resistance—the village of indomitables—and I doubted there could be any survivors.

A wave of exhaustion broke over me. I asked myself if this was all worth it, if I wasn't too young, too weak to endure it, this sordid chaos which seemed bent on invading my existence. I wanted to fall asleep and never wake up. Then I got cold. It was as dumb as that. I got cold and wanted to go inside. I took my mother by the arm and brought her into the house. She, too, was exhausted, certainly more than me. I wondered how she managed to bear up. I sat her on the couch, where she continued sobbing. I turned on the TV to keep her company and I went to see Sam in the trophy room. He was sitting on the floor, close to the hyena, hunched over his Game Boy. From that position, there was no way he could not have heard my mother's screams.

"Why did you do that?"

He didn't look up from his console.

"Why did I do what?"

"You know very well."

He made no reply.

"Didn't you hear Mom screaming?"

"I had my Walkman on."

I kicked him hard in the thigh. It made a thud. He laughed.

He had gotten bigger. His skinny body looked like a large bird. A vulture. His hair was darker too. He was letting it grow. It made him look a bit Seventies—totally dorkish. Despite it all, he was still a handsome kid. Particularly his eyes, with their supernatural green. He looked like a Stephen King hero. I wondered what kind of boy he would have been now if the ice-cream man hadn't had his accident.

I looked at the stuffed animals all around us. He seemed to belong to their family. A specimen of a young human among the specimens of other species. Absorbed by his game, he seemed to have already forgotten I was there.

I went back downstairs to see my mother. She was still on the couch. She had stopped sobbing. Listless, her arms folded across her chest, she rocked back and forth, moaning. On the TV, an ad was extolling the merits of a brand of ground beef. I switched it off. It was at this moment that my father came home from his day at work. I explained what had happened.

"Well it has to be a dog. The degenerates in the neighborhood don't know how to train their critters."

"No it's not a dog. A dog doesn't rip ears off, a dog doesn't torture. And above all, a dog doesn't leave such a clean cut on the neck."

This was the first time I had stood up to my father and his face told me I had just committed a serious error. My mother snapped out of her listlessness.

"Your father knows what he's saying, after all. He's used to this, he sees dead animals all the time."

"But he hasn't even seen it!"

"It's a dog, I'm telling you."

End of story.

My father buried Cumin's remains in Little Gallows Wood.

* * *

I had lied to my father in telling him I wanted to earn money to get Sam a gift for his birthday. So I needed to find him one. I had no idea what. Anything he'd be likely to appreciate risked nourishing the miasmas in his head. I had observed him closely in the days that followed Cumin's slaughter. He had lapped up every drop of my mother's pain. She wandered about the house, as lost and as helpless as a cat that had lost her kittens. Sometimes she made these whining sounds when her sorrow became unbearable. They escaped from her like jets of steam from a pressure cooker. She tried to contain them as best she could, but the pressure was too strong. In the end this riled my father, who growled, "Enough now, enough of this sentimentality," and he made that movement with his jaw. My mother didn't fail to notice it, and her terror stifled her grief. Sam had tasted her suffering, though. He watched my mother, mesmerized. His lips slackened, his neck arched, and he sucked up each gushing tear like a leech. In the end I gave him Donkey Kong, a new game for his Game Boy. At least when he was playing video games he wasn't harming anyone.

THE RAIN EVENTUALLY ceased and, when fall came, I returned to school and moved up a class. The other pupils were a year older than me, but I still viewed them as an army of cruel and frivolous morons. They sniffed each other's behinds without daring to make a move. The girls were scared of being seen as sluts, and the boys as perverts, though they were simply organisms dazed by the cacophony of hormonal systems in full mutation. And there was no shame in that.

My school was a huge block of black concrete with a few trees planted around the edges. It kind of looked like the Demo a bit: the charm of a bunker surrounded by domesticated vegetation, a form of nature that was still tolerated but which had long since lost the battle. The classrooms were dotted with a few windows, as thin as arrow slits—so thin that a body couldn't have slipped through. They were a beautiful metaphor for the institution's educational system, a straitjacket that didn't even try to give the illusion of freedom. I appreciated the irony of the thing, at least it had the merit of being consistent. The straitjacket image was not so far from the reality. Teenagers packed behind their desks in rows like leeks, forced to spend their days listening to tired teachers. It felt almost like punishment. At any rate, we were far from the "pleasure of learning" and the "joy of knowledge" extolled by the head teacher in his speech at the start of every year.

I really couldn't tolerate sitting still. An hour with my ass on a chair was true torture, I needed to move about. I never sat down at Professor Pavlović's, I walked back and forth in the dining room, like an athlete before a track meet. It was as if knowledge required movement in order to lodge itself in the right place. My whole body was engaged in the learning process, and the older I got, the more aware I became of its existence and its complexity.

I consequently suffered in class. My body had no right to exist, and my famished mind was put on dry bread and water. So it escaped via the arrow-slit windows to go walk in the woods.

I fantasized about the Champion. He took me by the hand and looked at me, like he had looked at me the day of the yard sale, when I felt naked in the middle of the crowd. And I understood that he was giving me permission to touch him. My fingers started by lightly brushing his arm, at the point where his tattoo began. I had never had time to properly see what it depicted, but I imagined it was a big tribal symbol that mentioned me. My first name perhaps. As if he had been waiting for me his whole life, had had prescience of our meeting, and had engraved me in his epidermis before our paths even crossed. I knew that my body, too, was subject to its own deep hormonal soup, like other people's. And that this deep soup gave me the desire to reproduce, because that's how a species survives. And that I was no exception to this rule. And that thinking about the Champion created a kind of ersatz sex act. And that this released endorphins. And that they soothed my body a little. Until the next class.

* * *

Early the following summer, my father made an odd announcement. He had decided to do a night game with Sam and me. It was a thing he organized with his buddies in the gun club to toughen up the children and get them used to walking through the forest in the dark. "It might happen at any moment, I won't give you any warning, you must be ready." He gave us each a little backpack containing a water bottle, a waterproof poncho, binoculars, a few cereal bars, and an Opinel clasp knife. This backpack had to stay beside our bed, ready to be grabbed in the middle of the night, along with a sweater, jeans, and a pair of walking shoes.

I didn't understand why he was making me take part in one of their activities, but I was happy to be allowed into their circle for once, even though the idea of finding myself in the middle of the woods at night with my father and brother terrified me. I knew that the hyena wouldn't be far and that she'd be stalking me closely. I went to bed each night, fear knotting my stomach, listening out for the slightest movement in the house. Dovka slept peacefully at my feet, with no inkling of the lurking threat. I envied her carefreeness. I would only fall asleep late into the night, when I was sure nobody would come drag me from my bed.

* * *

Sam had flunked his end-of-year tests. He showed not the slightest interest in school. He showed not the slightest interest in anything except death. I think that he was now almost incapable of feeling. His emotion-making mechanism was broken. And the only means of feeling was to kill or torture. I suppose that something happens when you kill. You change the position of a piece within the universe's great equilibrium and that generates a super-powerful feeling. Sam was bored. I knew that I would succeed in changing the past one day, but it would take time, and meanwhile my little brother's life was going to be a long, monotonous freeway strewn with animal carcasses.

My own life was quite different. I had goals. And even moments of intense joy. Each of my sessions with Professor Pavlović was a walk on a new planet belonging only to me and on which the hyena did not exist. And when I wasn't at the professor's, I continued to visit this planet by working on my own. I practiced relentlessly, dissecting the most complex equations and reading articles by contemporary researchers in scientific journals. Sometimes I even managed to surprise Professor Pavlović with research results he didn't know about. I dreamed of joining these teams who were experimenting with the laws of temporality. I clearly wasn't the only one dreaming of time travel and I was impatient to be able to meet these "others" who were crazy enough to dream of it too. I thought about Marie Curie a lot. She was my companion, always there in my head, and we talked to each other. I imagined her watchful, maternal eye on me all the time. I convinced myself in the end that, from her place in the kingdom of the dead, she had decided to become a kind of godmother to me. She espoused my cause.

Professor Pavlović didn't like the idea of time travel. But he was one of those scientists who maintained it was possible. The community was divided on this point. Stephen Hawking, for example, suggested that if time travel were conceivable, then we should already have been visited by travelers from the future. The fact that such visits hadn't happened proved the impossibility of temporal exploration. I thought this was a dishonest argument. Supposing someone did succeed, I had trouble imagining the people from the future showing up in flip-flops and Hawaiian shirts to play tourist in the 1990s. And then there were enough unexplained phenomena—attributed by the more naïve to extraterrestrial visits—that one couldn't exclude the very real existence of travelers from the future. At any rate, Professor Pavlović maintained that such an invention was theoretically conceivable, but that it was one of those continents of science it would be better not to explore. He said, "Time travel is like immortality: it's an understandable fantasy, but one must learn to accept the unacceptable. Man wants to understand, it's in his nature, his childish nature. Observe, understand, explain, that's your job as a scientist. But don't intervene. The universe has its laws, it works, it's a system that builds itself, at once designing, manipulating, and producing; you'll never be smarter than it. I tried before you, I know what I'm talking about." But if he had known Sam before the accident with the ice-cream man, he would never have said such a thing. There are some things you can't accept. Otherwise you die. And I didn't want to die. I was beginning to glimpse the beautiful things you can experience when you don't have a faceless man in your head.

* * *

Professor Pavlović had been an eminent physicist, recognized by the scientific community for his work on general relativity. But he had lost his credibility because of a theory on the dispersion of bodies that he had never been able to prove. If a body could be disintegrated then recomposed, that would make ideas such as time travel or teleportation possible, the professor was convinced of it. He claimed that this happened to us under particular circumstances, notably at the moment of orgasm. Each atom in the human body would be dispersed to the four corners of the universe, resulting in the total disintegration of the subject for an extremely short unit of time. Then everything would return to its place. The phenomenon would occur over a duration in the order of an attosecond, that is to say a quintillionth of a second. Impossible to measure. He also put forward the hypothesis that the more powerful the orgasm, the longer the phenomenon's duration would be.

The challenge was that in order to prove the validity of his theory, one would have to achieve an orgasm of atomic force in a body covered with spectroscopic sensors in order to observe the phenomenon of disintegration.

Needless to say, this theory made him the mockery of his colleagues. He had published several articles on the subject in specialist journals, but every one of his funding applications had been laughed out of town by the relevant committees. Since then, he sulked in his corner, refusing offers of professorships at the university. Yet I sensed that there was a part of him that hoped one day to have his revenge on the scientific community. And perhaps his revenge was me.

I SAW THE Champion several times over the summer. Sometimes I ran into him in the Demo on my way to Professor Pavlović's or while out walking Dovka.

And then came that evening.

He had asked me to come look after the kids. Usually it was Feather Girl who called me. But he was all on his own this time, since she had gone to spend a few days with her mother, in the South. He needed my help. The evening went well, as it always did. The kids were now three and one. It was the turn of little Yumi to have growing pains. But Takeshi asked me for a massage, too, so I organized a whole spa session in their bedroom, addressing them as "Mr. Takeshi" and "Madam Yumi":

"Would you care for a little herbal tea in your bottle?"

"Is the temperature of the oil to your liking?"

"Oh excuse me! I tickled you, that was quite unintentional!"

I had only to lightly press their milky little thighs between thumb and forefinger to make them squeal with laughter. I put them to bed much too late, but I needed this warmth they purveyed.

When they finally fell asleep, I didn't feel like turning on the TV—I hadn't been able to stand it for a while now, I think it reminded me too much of my father, and the smell of whisky. So I wandered around the house, examining every detail, every book, every object, every photo, playing at making deductions about their life together, their tastes, their habits. I smiled upon seeing the Sega Mega Drive, with the game Mortal Kombat II inside. The children were too young to play it. There was one controller plugged into the console and another lying on a shelf, covered in a fine layer of dust. It must have been a long time since the Champion and Feather Girl last played it together.

The bookshelf held a whole mixture of

things: Agatha Christie, Margaret Atwood, John Fante, Dean Koontz, Jane Austen, Victor Hugo, Jean-Marc Reiser, Alan Moore, Emile Zola, George Sand, Alexandre Dumas, Danielle Steele. And another book hidden behind the others: *The Sexuality of Married Couples: How to Keep the Flame Alive*. I lingered over it, knowing full well I had no right. There were tips such as "Surprise your partner," "Make love everywhere except in the marital bed," "Break with routine," "Go away for the weekend," "Use objects." There were notes in the margins, in a handwriting I guessed was Feather Girl's. Indeed, most of the tips seemed aimed at women: "Wear sexy lingerie," "Try full-body depilation." There was an illustrated chapter with diagrams. And a little booklet at the end with a game: every page had a drawing of a couple in a different position, and the aim was to open it at random and copy what you saw there. Feather Girl had marked certain pages with a cross. I wondered if it was to show what she preferred or what she didn't. I was so absorbed in my reading that I didn't hear the Champion's car. Suddenly I felt his presence. I gave a little scream of surprise. He stood next to the couch, his muscular body packed into his tight jeans and white T-shirt, his keys in his hand. His face was scarlet, though I couldn't tell if it was from embarrassment or anger. He simply said, "Put that back, please." I don't think he was really angry, but the air in the room had taken on a peculiar consistency. It was thick, as if each movement of ours shifted large quantities of matter. I put the book back, saying, "Sorry, I ..." Then I stepped toward him and toward the door.

"I can get home on my own, you don't have to take me." He seemed caught off-guard. He hesitated for a few seconds before replying.

"OK. All good?"

"Yeah, yeah. Very good."

When I stepped past him to leave, he grabbed my wrist.

"Hang on."

He smelled of drink. But not my father's whisky, something much lighter. Beer, probably.

"I won't say anything to her about the book. That's just between us."

My wrist was still in his hand.

"OK. Thanks."

The air was so thick, it had trouble entering my lungs. My body had never been this close to the Champion's. I knew now that the throbbing down there, between my legs, was my own carnal desire calling to his.

I reminded myself that I was simply in the flawed offshoot of my life. So I could try anything now, there was no real risk. One day I would go back in time. I would return to that summer evening when I was ten years old, and none of this would ever have happened. So I moved closer. I could smell his breath. It was beer alright. My lips touched his cheek. If they had withdrawn straightaway, as fast as they had come, it would have been an innocent kiss goodbye. But like two magnets brought far too close together, our lips found each other. I kissed that mouth which, a few years earlier, had hollered "You piece of shit!" at the drunk. Now it murmured, "What are you doing?" My only answer was to kiss him harder. So my lips opened and the Champion's tongue caressed them, quite gently. His arms closed around my body, pulling me against him. I felt as fragile as a matchstick. His mouth slipped down to my neck, and his hands moved up to my shoulders, then back down again, to my breasts. His breathing changed, becoming more intense, the pressure of his hands stronger. Suddenly he grabbed my shoulders and pushed me away. "No. Go home."

He wouldn't look at me. But I didn't want to leave him. I inhaled his silence. Then my gaze rose to his chin, and my lips pounced on his; yet it didn't seem like a conscious decision. I couldn't imagine a force strong enough to separate us, and I couldn't see why what was happening at this moment was forbidden. I loved him. And he loved me in a certain way, I was sure of it. Period. His tongue caressed my mouth again, he sighed, then his hands pushed me away once more.

"Stop!"

His voice was firmer this time. He looked at me. There was something beseeching in his eyes. I made a superhuman effort and stepped away from him and left the house.

The night was bright out in the Demo. I felt that something was calling me far from here. There was an energy filling me, an energy that could take me someplace else and make me achieve miracles. I wanted to run, with a mixture of joy and impatience. But for now I had to go home. Close to my father, my mother, my brother, and to death. I walked back to my house and went in. My father was alone on the couch, sitting on his bear pelt in the dark, his face lit by the TV's bluish light. I went upstairs without a sound.

I had no desire to sleep. I almost hoped that the night game would happen right there and then, for I felt capable of facing anything.

When I got undressed to go to bed, I noticed an unusual smell coming from my vagina. The smell of pleasure. I fell asleep in the Champion's arms. I had such fierce desire for his presence that I could feel his body against mine. He was sleeping only a few yards away from me. Alone.

* * *

My father had never mentioned this night-game business again, so I ended up believing he'd forgotten. Nevertheless, I remained alert every night, listening out for the slightest creak in the silent house.

The oak tree outside my window still threw its menacing shadow. Sometimes the wind shook the shadow, and the branches danced a macabre waltz at the foot of my bed. I watched this tawdry ballet, my body tense, my heart thumping with anxiety, waiting for my bedside clock to show "03:00" before I fell asleep.

One night, around late August, it finally happened. It was precisely 00:12. There was movement in my parents' room, then I heard my father's heavy step in the hall. The door of my room opened. "It's time," he growled. I dressed quickly, watched curiously by Dovka. T-shirt, hoodie, jeans, stout shoes, my backpack. Dovka wanted to follow me, but I told her "no," so she went back and lay on my bed. I didn't yet realize quite how much I would envy her over the course of this night.

Sam was already waiting down in the hallway. My father scrutinized me as I descended the stairs, as if examining every part of my body. Like he was wondering which bit he would choose to nail to a wooden board on his wall of trophies. I realized that I shouldn't follow them, that I shouldn't go into that forest with them. But I had no choice. Nobody had asked my opinion.

We stepped out into the night and got into my father's 4×4. He drove for an hour, toward the trees, toward the vast forest, which could swallow you up for mile after square mile, and where some said wolves now roamed again.

There wasn't a cloud in the sky. As we drew away from the lights of the human world, the stars appeared like so many thousands of spectators taking their seats to watch a show. I knew neither my own role nor that of the other characters, only that I should not step onto this stage.

The road grew narrower as it cut through the forest, into the heart of darkness, the pines towering all around us like sentinels. I had the sensation they were waiting for me. After several miles on the narrow road, the car turned off onto a dirt track that sloped gently down into the depths of the night. The moon's weak glow faded away behind the treetops, plunging the ground into impenetrable obscurity, out of which loomed tree trunks picked out by the headlight beams—like giants ready to smash us. I told myself that if a predator were roaming these woods, it would have no difficulty in spotting us from afar. Our bright headlights made us a clear target.

We reached a clearing, in which two other 4×4s were waiting for us, along with two men and three boys. As he got out of the car, my brother headed straight over to the boys. I figured they must be his buddies from the shooting range. This was the first time I'd seen my brother display friendship to anyone since the ice-cream man's accident. He even seemed to consider them playmates. A fierce anger seeped into my chest. Filthy little jerk. That he didn't want to play with me was one thing, but to be having fun with other kids at the same time, that made me want to punch him in the face. After all I'd done for him! Then I remembered that it wasn't him. Just the miasmas swarming through his skull, turning it into a little cloud buzzing with slimy spurts and mangled bones.

The men slapped each other on the back and shook hands. This was also the first time I had seen my father in a social setting outside of our family circle. Sam and he were letting me catch a glimpse of their world, and in a way I was flattered. Two of the boys were brothers, they must have been ten and twelve. They were wiry and tough. In their black ᴛ-shirts, they made me think of a couple of riding crops. Their words rang out, clean and precise. Nothing vague, nothing extraneous. The younger one cast me a brief glance. I could tell he had scanned me. He would go over the details later, in his own time. The older of the two was the center of attention as he showed off the rifle he'd just been given. I knew nothing about this stuff, but it was apparently an exceptional weapon, judging by the others' admiring exclamations.

The third boy was the precise opposite of the first two. Where everything about them suggested rigor and discipline, this one seemed to have grown up wonky, according to the vagaries of his whims. He was pale and podgy, as if he'd been incubated in a Coke bottle. He talked loudly, telling his father that he wanted "the same gun." Actually no, he didn't tell, he ordered. And the father laughed nervously as he explained that it really did cost an awful lot, though he already knew he'd lost.

The father of the two riding crops looked at this third boy with a mixture of pity and disgust. He himself had every appearance of a dog trainer. I half-expected him to pull out an ultrasonic whistle to communicate with his sons. But the leader of the gang was my father, that was clear. Probably thanks to the elephant tusk. I suppose that, in the hunting world, the leader was the one who had killed the biggest animal. Or the largest number. In either case, my father was undoubtedly the winner.

"Right, kids," he said, "you got your gear?"

"Yes!" we all replied.

"Tonight, you will undertake your first tracking. Tracking is ..."

You'd have thought he was recalling the memory of a love affair.

"It's the moment when the link is woven between you and the animal. A unique link. You'll see that it's the animal who decides. There will come a moment when the animal offers itself to you because you are the strongest. It capitulates. And that's when you shoot. It requires patience, you must harry your prey until it decides that it prefers death. You will see that it's neither your eyes nor your ears that guide you to your prey, but your hunter's instinct. Your own soul communes with the animal's and then you simply have to let your steps lead you to it, quite calmly, without rushing. If you are true killers, then it should be easy.

"There will be no killing tonight, however. Just the tracking. And the prey will be ..."

My blood ran cold as he turned to me.

"... you."

THE FOUR BOYS sniggered.

"The aim is not to hurt her. She is my daughter, after all, and I'd like to marry her off one day, ha! ha! ha! So don't damage her. The killing will be symbolized by a small lock of her hair. And I mean a small one, no need to hack it all off, just a strand will do. The first to bring me one wins."

"No, dad!" I protested, "I don't want to do it! I don't!"

* * *

His jaw made that weird movement and I understood why he had that look when I came downstairs an hour and a half earlier: the hyena's blood flowed in his veins, and my imploring delighted him. He was almost licking his lips.

"Run," he said, in his deep voice, "you get a five-minute head start."

"Dad, please, stop."

My eyes smarted with tears, and my throat was seized with choking sobs.

My father started the chronometer on his wristwatch.

"You're losing time."

I looked at the others: the two riding crops, their father, the little fat kid, and his father. They were waiting for me to take to my heels. My gaze met Sam's. He smiled his cruel smile, the one that stank. Filthy son of a bitch. I wanted to scream. I wanted to tear out his horrid little shitty eyes, plunge my hands in all the way, extract the infection from his head, and smash it to death with my fists while yelling "You piece of shit!" as the Champion had done with Derek's dad. I heard the hyena's laugh. It echoed everywhere, in my head, in the forest, in the black sky of this warm summer heavy with the smell of an oncoming storm—it should have been so beautiful.

I didn't cry. I told myself I mustn't. Not cry. Not give the hyena that gift again. I turned my back on them and ran. The obvious direction was back the way we came, following the dirt track to the road. There I'd stop the first car, which would take me to the nearest village, and from there I could think what to do. But after a few yards I realized that I'd have to wait much longer than five minutes for a car to pass by on this deserted little road in the middle of the woods. And I'd be out in the open, an easy prey. So I turned toward the forest, as dark and thick as a sea of tar. The key thing was to disappear, get as far away from my pursuers as possible. I could return to the road later; for now, I had to flee. I ran so fast that I couldn't tell where I was placing my feet. The more I ran, the clearer my role as prey became, and the more I panicked. I felt like I was flying. The carpet of dead pine needles rustled beneath my feet. I held my arms out in front of me to protect my face from the branches, which I couldn't see in the darkness and which seemed to want to poke my eyes out. I prayed I wouldn't run into a barbwire fence. I hadn't the slightest idea what direction to take, so I continued straight ahead, as fast as my legs would allow. The trees seemed never-ending; I felt

I could have run like that for days before encountering any semblance of civilization.

I reached the foot of a steep slope around thirty feet high. Climbing it would slow me down. I told myself that once at the top I would not only have a good outlook over the others, but it would be a safe place to hide out before attempting to get back to the road. And anyhow, I couldn't continue running at this speed very much longer. Panic compressed my throat, and my lungs were on fire. I had no means of measuring the time that had passed since my father started his stopwatch, but something told me that we weren't far off the five minutes. As if in answer to my question, a cry pierced the night somewhere behind me. I couldn't make out the precise word. It sounded vaguely like "Gooooooooo!" and I figured that it must have been the signal to start the hunt, like when Sam and I played hide-and-go-seek in the car boneyard. Blood buzzed in my ears as I scrambled up the last few feet separating me from the top of the slope and threw myself against a thick tree trunk. In the darkness, my body and the tree's could be easily confused. I tried to get my breath back as silently as possible, but my throat whistled. The air had all the trouble in the world penetrating my trachea, which had closed to a tiny hole, compressed by exertion, terror, and sobbing. I felt despair overwhelm me, as floods of tears rose to my eyes, threatening to turn me into a little, hiccoughing ball on its bed of thorns. But then my anger stepped in, beating down on the floods of tears like an incandescent sun. My despair dried away and something hardened inside of me. The air began flowing through my trachea normally again.

I listened carefully to try and ascertain the position of my pursuers, but all I heard were the sounds of the forest. Some kind of owl hooted a few yards away from me. The wind shook the branches. Otherwise the night was wrapped in a silence that was both reassuring and disturbing. I weighed up the situation. If I remained hidden there, without moving, I couldn't see how they were going to be able to find me. As terrifying as it might be, the darkness was my best ally. No one could hear or see me unless they were less than six feet from the tree I was clutching. But right then it hit me, with all the subtlety of a semi-trailer truck: from the point at which I had turned off the dirt track, I had run straight ahead. My pursuers only had to follow the direction I had taken from where they had seen me disappear between the trees and it would take them straight to me, at the top of the slope. Why hadn't I thought to change direction as I ran?! What a dumbass! She understands quantum physics, but isn't even capable of a little cunning in the face of a bunch of prepubescent hunters!

I needed to preserve my head start by continuing on as stealthily as possible, and just hope that my steps would guide me out of this forest. I got up, turning my back to the slope. My first step on the mixture of pine needles and dry branches tore the silence apart with a sinister crunch. I imagined all the predators in the region pricking up their ears and pointing their muzzles in my direction. But I figured that if I was going to break the silence, I might as well maintain my lead, so I started running again. At least little fatso wouldn't catch me.

I settled into my stride, trying to forget that I was a young girl lost in the forest in the depths of the night, pursued by a pack of unpredictable maniacs who wanted to cut off my hair. I tried to forget the menacing shadows of the trees, which I imagined coming to life at every moment to pierce my flesh with their long, spiky fingers.

I ran for a long time, so long that my legs became painful. And I started to get thirsty. I spotted a dead tree trunk, inside which I huddled down, in total darkness. I slipped off my backpack, put it on my lap, and opened the zipper without a sound. As I felt around inside for my flask, my blood ran cold. Apart from the flask and the cereal bars, my bag was empty. Someone had taken out the poncho, the binoculars, and the Opinel knife. During all those insomniac nights, I had never thought to check its contents. The backpack had been safe in my room, at the foot of my bed. There was no way that ...

My father.

I imagined him entering my room to purloin these three objects, and the image terrified me. Because it made all too real the idea that he had decided from the get-go that I would be the prey. He had no doubt been savoring this prospect for weeks. I swallowed several large mouthfuls of water, trying to drown the sobs that were again clawing their way up my throat. My anger gave way and the burning streams poured down my cheeks. I stayed there, crying silently in the dead tree trunk for a few minutes.

I was just thinking about putting my flask away and running on when a noise made me jump. A sharp CLACK. It came from close by, barely a few yards from where I was. Someone had struck something hard.

My body withdrew beneath the tree trunk, like an oyster under a squirt of vinegar. I stopped breathing. Someone was standing there, quite close, on the other side of the trunk. I couldn't see them, but I felt them. I remembered my father's words. "Your own soul communes with the animal's and then you simply have to let your steps lead you to them, quite calmly, without rushing."

My soul was communing with that of another, a killer. He had found me. The hyena had found me. I had forgotten that one couldn't hide from her. She was in everything, everywhere, under the skin of the world, and she had decided to come sniff me with her monstrous snout, here, in the forest, far from the tribe of men, from Feather Girl and the Champion, from Professor Pavlović.

I closed my eyes, waiting to be discovered. It was only a matter of seconds. And maybe that wasn't a bad thing. The game would end and I'd be free and clear, all for a lock of hair. I just wanted it to stop, and to go home to my bed and be with Dovka.

But whatever was on the other side of the trunk had no desire to interrupt the game. Terror flowed from my soul to its own, and it lapped it up. I was certain that it was neither the three kids nor their fathers. It was my brother or my father, or something else entirely ... and I didn't know which of these three ideas horrified me the most. I heard rough breathing. Or was it the wind setting the tops of the big oaks a-creaking? The thing drew nearer, leaned down against the trunk, and sniffed at the surface of my skin. Eyes closed, I felt its breath in my hair. I imagined a misshapen head, swollen with hate, black fangs bristling from its reptilian maw; a phosphorescent gaze. The thing pondered. The fusty traces of its decomposed soul rose to the surface of its consciousness in fat fetid bubbles. Then it stood back up and withdrew, replete. It took me several minutes to be capable of rational thought again. I had to get out of this forest as quickly as possible.

I listened. Silence had enveloped the night once more like a dark velvet drape. I was alone, an idea that reassured me as much as it horrified me. My body relaxed and I decided to pull myself out of my hidey hole. That's when I felt the pain. I had thrown myself so hard against the tree trunk that a stump of branch had stuck into my back. My brain, blinded by terror, hadn't noticed it at the time. I felt beneath my T-shirt. Holding my hand up, I saw the red on my fingers in the moonlight. It can't have been that serious, barely more than a graze, but the sight of my blood brought tears to my eyes again.

I tried to calculate how much time there was before dawn. This would all be more bearable in the light of day. And anyway, I figured this stupid game would end once the sun rose. I didn't even know how they intended on finding me. It must have been 01:30 when the starting signal was given. Daybreak was around six in the morning this time of year. I just needed to know how much time had passed since I'd started running through this forest. Thirty minutes? An hour? No more. I therefore had over three hours of darkness to contend with. It was out of the question to wait for daybreak. I would get going again and I would get myself out of here. If I ran in the same direction, I should be able to exit this forest fairly rapidly. The idea comforted me a little. My pulse returned to a normal rhythm. I even started to wonder if my imagination hadn't played tricks on me and if I hadn't imagined the predator. After all, the only noise I'd heard was that CLACK. Sure, it had startled me, but perhaps it was just a rotten branch giving way and crashing to the forest floor. Indeed, had I even really heard it at all?

I asked myself this as I adjusted the straps of my backpack, preparing to run again, when terror slapped me, drawing a scream. I stood rooted to the ground, petrified. A few yards in front of me, half lit by a moon-beam, a figure stood out, quite still, against the thick trunk of a pine tree. I remained frozen for a few seconds, eyes fixed on what was standing before me. I couldn't make out its face, hidden by a hood. A cawing filled the sky. Something about the figure's stillness terrified me maybe more than its presence—it suggested that fleeing wouldn't do me any good, that it was sure to catch me, whatever I might try. I continued to stare, waiting for it to make a decision. I was intrigued by the wind, which made the figure move like a ghostly creature. I drew a little closer and saw that it was not a person, but a khaki rain poncho. My own poncho, pinned to the bark with my Opinel clasp knife. A second scream stayed in my belly. Whoever had done this couldn't be far away. It was even probable that they were watching me right now, concealed in the shadows. I could feel their gaze on the back of my neck and it had the effect on me of a fistful of teeming worms struggling to penetrate my skin.

My legs began to run, without asking my say-so, strides hammering across the ground. I had no idea where I was going, I simply had to escape all this, run right across the planet, enter another world, it didn't matter. I wasn't a prey, for fucksake. Never that. Yet I was acting like one, bolting through the forest, my gut burning with panic.

I ran so fast that I didn't notice the terrain changing beneath my feet. Sharp rocks began jutting through the carpet of pine needles. I stumbled once. Something inside of me, my good sense probably, told me to slow down, but fear was coursing through my veins, sweeping aside all rational thought.

My right foot hit a big rock and then my body was in the air. I had time to understand that I was too high, that I was traveling too fast, and that I couldn't do anything to avoid the impact.

I HIT THE ground horizontally. A rock struck me just below my breasts. I felt a *crack* inside. "Oh, a rib!" I said to myself with a spectator's lucidity. My right hand slipped between my face and a sharp pebble. But my palm didn't scream when the stone punctured it, it was braver than me. I lay there for a few seconds, unable to move, the pebble in my hand, the rock digging into my side. The pain bored through my chest, radiating down to my toes. I had never hurt so much.

That's when it hatched. In the pit of my stomach. Not in my gut, much deeper than that, beyond everything. A creature much bigger than me was growing in my belly. It wasn't that warm, soft beast nurtured by the Champion. This one was hideous, its wretched face spewing other creatures, its offspring. This beast wanted to devour my father, and all those who wanted to harm me. This beast forbade me to cry. It let out a long roar that ripped the night apart. And everything changed. I was a prey no more. A predator neither. I was me and I was indestructible.

I stood up, dry-eyed. My broken rib was tearing me in two, and I had trouble breathing. There was a deep gash in my hand, from which blood ran in a continuous stream. Usually when I hurt myself, my initial reflex was to lick the wound, but there was too much blood this time. I took off my hoodie, then my T-shirt to make a compress. Each movement felt like a knife stabbed into my ribcage. I put my hoodie back on, then my backpack, and wrapped my T-shirt around my hand.

I thought about going back for my Opinel knife stuck in the tree, before telling myself that I was so full of rage, and that the creature had spewed so many little ones, that if I was attacked I would be capable of killing with my bare hands. As I started walking again, I wished from the darkest folds of my soul for someone to appear and attempt to cut a strand of my hair. They'd see, alright. I'd smash their filthy little face in.

I carried on walking like that for a while, I couldn't say how long. But the further I walked, the more intense the pain in my side became. I could hardly feel the pain in my hand anymore, so excruciating was the agony compressing my chest, making it very hard to breathe. According to what I'd learned in science class, this must have been due to the diminishing quantity of endorphins in my body, rendering the pain signal increasingly perceptible.

My rage had calmed a little, but I was no longer afraid, and I still felt indestructible. I stopped to drink a little water, and forced myself to eat a cereal bar, too, because I had lost a lot of blood. Not enough to put my life in danger, but sufficient to cause slight anemia. The idea of losing consciousness in the middle of this forest was unbearable.

I was just putting the empty cereal bar wrapper in my jeans pocket when something drew my attention far away below me to my left. A little moving glimmer. Headlights. Car headlights. And they seemed to be getting closer. I began walking again, as fast as my rib would allow, hoping I would reach the road I figured lay in front of me before the car passed by. It didn't seem to be driving too fast, so I ought to make it. I hurried on through the bracken. The terrain sloped down steeply into darkness. My abdomen was screaming, but the prospect of getting out of this forest was stronger than the pain. I stepped over several thorny thickets, scratching my calves as I did so.

The car was still approaching and seemed to be driving in my direction. I reached the bottom of the slope, placing my feet on a ground I couldn't see, strewn with brambles. I tripped and fell on my hands, feeling a nettle sting, but compared with what I was suffering, it was no worse than a kitten mewing. I picked myself up and covered the few yards left between me and the road.

Where I expected to feel asphalt beneath my feet, I found only packed dirt. It wasn't a road but a track, like the one we'd taken a few hours earlier. (How long ago? One hour? Two hours? Four? I no longer had the slightest idea.) But the headlights were real alright, and they were approaching. I was now bang in the middle of their beams, such that the driver must have seen me. And indeed the car slowed, then stopped a few yards away. It remained motionless for around ten seconds, as if looking at me. Dazzled by the headlights, I could see neither the car nor its occupants, but this wait augured nothing good. Finally they cut the engine, and the driver and passenger doors opened at the same time. Two people got out. I didn't dare approach. The two figures came forward, silhouetted in the headlights' glare.

Little fatso and his dad.

Walking through the forest must have tired the boy. Or terrorized him. He had preferred to continue the hunt by 4×4.

I didn't feel like fleeing them, because I was in pain, because I wasn't scared, and because my hideous creature was bent on destruction. The kid was a good head taller than me and forty-five pounds heavier, but what I felt at that instant was simply impatience. To feel his face crumple under my knuckles.

I waited for him, motionless.

Little fatso walked toward me hesitantly, a pair of scissors in his hand. He attempted a "We found you, you lost!" but there was a touch of anxiety in his voice. He approached cautiously, as if he had been ordered to stroke a wild animal. Dazzled by the headlights, I could only make out his dark hulk, but I could smell his sweaty forehead and his fat quivering cheeks.

When he was a few inches from me, he raised his hand to my hair. I waited for him to touch me. I savored this wait. The tips of his fingers brushed a blonde strand. And the beast lunged, like a bullet exiting the barrel of a rifle. My fist struck his cheekbone with such force, it knocked him flat on the dirt track. I threw myself on him, the beast roaring from the farthest depths of my bowels, accompanied by a bloodthirsty army of Vikings. I hit him so hard, I thought I would puncture his skull. And though I was punching him with my injured hand, I felt nothing.

The kid screamed: "Daaaaaaaaad!"

I was able to hit him for a few seconds longer, then a hand yanked me by the hair. My legs propelled me backward and I bit the first thing I could. An arm. I clamped my jaws so tight that I felt the flesh give between my teeth. The father grabbed me tightly round the neck with his free hand, and I had to let go of his arm.

He tackled me to the ground, shifting my fractured rib. I screamed in pain. My head was immobilized by his hands, but my body still struggled and writhed, kicking my legs in all directions.

"Help me, for god's sake!" the father roared at his son. The kid got up then sat astride my stomach, his knee pressing into my side. The agony was so extreme, I could no longer breathe at all.

"Grab her hands."

They both set upon me, pinning me to the ground with all their hostility, as pointless as that now was, for I had stopped moving, stifled by the pain. I was beaten. I heard the "shlik" of the scissors in my hair. They let go of me, the father and son, and rushed back to the safety of their 4×4, leaving me lying there, alone, in the middle of the track.

The sound of a foghorn boomed out. It must have been the signal that the game was over.

The son got back out of the car and the

father reversed away to make it look like the kid had pulled off this feat on his own, like a big boy. Darkness cloaked around us again. I remained on the ground, raging against myself and against my creature that wasn't strong enough to protect me. Little fatso began sobbing, a few yards from me. I'd hurt him with my fists. We stayed like that for several long minutes, him sat on the verge, whimpering, me lying on the dirt track, stomaching my defeat.

I stood up when I heard the others approaching; I didn't want them to see a vanquished animal. The kid dried his tears with the back of his hand and victoriously brandished the lock of my hair. The two riding crops, who arrived first, didn't hide their resentment. Judging by the look on their father's face, those two were in line for a few extra sessions of harsh training.

My brother arrived shortly after. He took in the blood-red T-shirt wrapped around my hand. For once, I didn't see the vermin hordes in his gaze. Quite the opposite, I saw that he wasn't OK with all this, that the game had gone too far. He looked at little fatso and his hands tensed. The village of

indomitables gave a cry of revolt from beyond the valleys of wilderness and swamps.
He wasn't dead. Thank goodness.

Dawn was starting to stain the black sky
with purplish blue. I understood from my
brother's gaze that I should continue to
fight. Without him, that night would have
swallowed all my will.

I was unsure what attitude to adopt as
regards my father. On one hand I wanted to
make him comprehend that I was no prey,
that I was not my mother, that I was not
empty inside, that a beast lived there, a
beast one should be wary of approaching.
But I also told myself that if I wasn't up to
fighting a little spotty fatso and a man with
a will no firmer than pâté, I wasn't yet ready
to stand up to my father. And until I was, it
would doubtless be wiser to keep a low profile. So I lowered my gaze and took the attitude of a frightened little girl.

Little fatso's father had put on a jacket
over his T-shirt to hide the bite, which must
have been bleeding a bit, judging by the
lingering metallic taste on my tongue.

My father jerked his chin at my bloody
hand.

"You hurt yourself?"

"I fell on some rocks."

"Ha, ha! I swear! Letting a woman run around the woods on her own!"

Everyone laughed. Except Sam and me.

* * *

We drove home as we came, in silence.

My mother was already up when we got back. She was waiting for us in the hallway. I saw the look on her face as I stepped in the door. I must have been a frightening sight with my dirty clothes, my grazed face, and my bloody hand. She turned pale, her jaw dropped, then her gaze met my father's and she closed her mouth again. "Help her clean up," he told her, "She's managed to hurt herself."

Something told me that these words masked a touch of guilt. Maybe it was just a need to feel better, but I convinced myself that my father was not the monster who had come to sniff my fear beneath the tree trunk.

My mother took me to the bathroom. Since she was used to taking care of the animals, she knew what to do. She disinfected my hand, then made me take off my sweater. When she saw the scrape on my side, her eyes misted over and she brought her hand to her mouth. She was familiar with this pain. As the tears flowed, she handed me a pill and a glass of water, saying, "This'll help a bit." Her voice was choked. After giving me a hand with my pajamas, she helped me onto my bed, closed the curtains and sat there, waiting for me to fall asleep. She stroked my knee with her icy hand and, in the darkness, I heard her say:

"Earn some money and get out of here."

This was the first time she had given me any advice. Indeed it must have been the first time in her life that she had given advice to anyone.

"Mom, how come you failed in life?"

The words burst out before I had time to think or to hold them back. They surprised me so much that I wondered if I had really spoken them. Or if they came from someone else.

There was no malice in my question. It was a real question. My mother's life was a failure. I didn't know if there were such things as successful lives, nor what that could mean, but I knew that a life without laughter, without choices, and without love was a wasted life. I hoped for a reason, an explanation.

My mother's face cracked. It wasn't sorrow: tectonic plates had shuddered deep within her. Something had opened up in her desolate interior. Something which would change her internal chemistry. Something which would perhaps allow life to blossom. "Earn some money and get out of here," she said again. Then she just sat there, on the edge of my bed.

I laid my head on the pillow, seeking the least painful position in which to fall asleep. Eventually I realized that I would have no respite. That it would take weeks for my pain to go away, and that when it had gone, the fear would remain, I would never be free of it. But there was that thing growing deep inside of me that, when the situation demanded, was capable of sweeping away my terror and turning me into a predator.

My body felt a little soothed. The pill was

working. Dovka came and curled up in my arms. My mother wept softly. I listened to her sobbing for a few minutes, before falling into a bottomless sleep.

THE NEXT MORNING I had an appointment with Professor Pavlović. I would rather have died than not go. But every breath made me feel like I was being run through with a sword dipped in chili pepper.

As I walked across the Demo with Dovka, I tried to step as softly as I could to reduce the shock biting into each of my wounds. The cut on my hand throbbed. I knew it was my antibodies fighting the infection, and I hoped they would win. I knew all too well that if it became necessary to take me to hospital, this whole affair would take on proportions that my father would not appreciate. It was sunny. The parakeets squawked. The indifference of birds, forever and always.

* * *

Professor Pavlović opened the door. He stood there for a few seconds, without saying anything, taking in the grazes on my face and the dressing around my hand, on which a dark red stain had spread during the night. Then, from beneath his thick eyebrows, he did something quite strange. Without moving, he took me in his arms. With his eyes.

Over his shoulder, the white mask appeared. Yael was mute, but she wasn't deaf. And her husband's silence had told her something unusual was happening. Dovka yapped. The mask's two black holes stared at me, exactly like Professor Pavlović had. I think I would have laughed, if Ya's mask hadn't scared me so much. They were amusing, the pair of them, like a couple of owls. But behind her plaster mouth painted red, Yael's real mouth, the one I'd never seen, the one I wasn't sure I'd ever want to see, gave a wail that froze the sun. A long, sinister scream, neither human nor animal. She spewed raw grief. An unfathomable pain that seemed to gush out after years of silence.

She screamed as if her vocal cords would

break. I think it was the most dreadful sound that had reverberated through the neighborhood since the explosion of the ice-cream seller's siphon. Professor Pavlović turned and took her by the shoulders.

"Ya!"

The scream didn't want to cease. He guided her to the small living room and helped her sit in the armchair. The mask continued to wail, louder and louder. There was more than pain now, fury too. This screaming hurt me. Even more than my rib. The professor tried to calm her.

"Breathe, Ya. Slowly."

He took her old hand in his old hand and stroked it, like a petrified baby rabbit. This scream was so visceral, so real, that for a moment I thought the mask would come to life. But it remained frozen, with its smile, its sequins, and its feathers.

"All's well, Ya. Calm down now."

It was disconcerting to see the professor try to comfort someone. He was always a little awkward with me; inaccessible actually. He expressed almost no emotion. Over time, I understood that it was a kind of shyness. He was incapable when it came to social interactions, for there was an element of the irrational in human relations. And Professor Pavlović did not understand the irrational. But Yael was different. She was his wife.

The wail wasn't weakening, so the professor opened a drawer and took out a syringe and a vial. Then, very gently, he grasped the arm marbled with rust-colored patches. These patches always intrigued me. They reminded me of the hands of the old ice-cream man. With age, I too would eventually rust up like an old fence.

The professor gave her the shot, and the voice faded. The mask was silent once more. Yael's head lolled back on a cushion and I realized that sleep had carried her away.

"Go wait for me in the dining room."

I knew he was going to remove her mask. As I made my way to the dining room I heard the sound of the radio, which the professor had just switched on. A classical-music station. I sat down at the table. The professor joined me. His thick black eyebrows were knitted so thickly that the space between them had disappeared completely. They now formed a thick, straight line across his forehead, like a Mars Bar. I stifled a nervous laugh. He sat down opposite me, stroked his goatee, and began rolling the bead between his fingers. His gaze was fixed on the chair to my right. It was like he was preparing to address it.

"Yael hasn't always been like that."

I realized we wouldn't be discussing physics today.

"We met at college, in Tel Aviv. She was studying medicine, and I physics. When she graduated she began working in a hospital. There she met many women who had issues with their husbands. Issues of violence. Both physical and psychological. She watched them arrive, with their bruises and their split lips, walking wrecks. And then, when they had recovered a bit, physically at least, they returned home and it started again. It drove Yael crazy. So she had a word with the hospital director, a decent guy. With his support, together they set up a shelter for battered women. She helped a lot of women, you know. She also got involved in feminist movements. She was a real activist. Me, I spent most of my time at the university. I was starting to teach while continuing my research.

"There was this woman, Lyuba. She had fled her home with her baby, a little boy no older than six months. Her husband, he ..."

He looked me straight in the eyes.

"He was the kind of guy it was better not to antagonize. He turned over all of Tel Aviv looking for his wife and baby. She needed to move far away, and quickly too. Yael helped her to make contact with her family in Russia, and to travel there. Lyuba and her son got away just in time, but the guy was furious. He made his investigations. Methodically. Until he found Yael."

His face was so tense that for a moment I thought it was going to split like dry wood.

"When Yael left the shelter one evening, he was waiting for her. With his buddies. And I wasn't there to protect her. The things they did to her that night ... The doctor's report, it said ..."

The dry wood split. Through the bark I saw a woman screaming. I saw the face pleading with the thing that had no name, before it disappeared. I saw the black wings and the red eyes.

"They took their time. It went on for

hours, all night. She remembered that they laughed, a lot. Particularly when they poured acid on her face." The bead continued to roll between his fingers.

"After that, they dumped her in front of the emergency room. They wanted her to survive so her torment would continue long afterward. And survive she did. Initially in a coma. I spent endless nights by her side, telling myself that if I truly loved her, I should unplug her respirator. Because no one can live without a face; without a nose or a mouth; without speaking or tasting. I nearly did it, countless times. But I just couldn't.

"The doctors succeeded in saving her right eye. The left one had literally dissolved. When she emerged from the coma, she took a piece of paper and a pen and wrote: 'Lyuba and the baby are well.' And I swear that, even without a mouth, she smiled. I realized she had won."

The professor stood up and went into the kitchen. I stayed there, listening to the strange silence that followed his tale. All I could hear was the sound of the radio from the living room. I imagined Yael sleeping, without a nose or a mouth, with a dissolved eye.

The professor returned carrying a steaming teapot. He sat down, poured the tea, and pushed a cup toward me.

"So, I don't know what happened to you, and I won't ask. But if there's anyone to be got rid of, know that Lyuba's husband made a good meal for the aquatic fauna of Tel Aviv Harbor."

From his silence, I understood that this was a question.

I shook my head.

"You don't want me to get involved?"

I shook my head again.

"Fine. Let's get down to work."

* * *

My mother took care of me as best she could, and she was pretty skilled at it. My hand didn't get infected. She applied poultices of green clay several times a day. The contact with the clay soothed me, as did my mother's ministrations. I saw her as an ally for the first time and I think it was reciprocal. For my rib, there was nothing to be done except relieve the pain while waiting for the bone to regenerate. I took the pain-killers my mother provided. I think it did her good to look after me. In fact I was sure of it. Maybe she suffered from feeling use-less most of the time. She needed to be needed, which would explain her passion for her goats, her plants, and her parakeet: all of them creatures who depended on her.

I resolved to ask for her help more often. To ask her for anything, actually, some-thing which I had never done before. I asked her for little things, such as help mending a zipper, or showing me how to set the alarm on my clock radio. I even realized that we shared an interest in science. She was more into biology, with her animals and her gar-den, but she had acquired a mass of quite impressive empirical knowledge, and I saw how surprised she was herself at the joy she took in sharing it with me.

Summer ended with this confusion of feelings: amazement at the connection being forged with the one I called "mom," and exponential terror induced by the one I called "dad."

FROM THE START of the following summer, I realized that my life was going to change. Radically. That year, the amusement park where my father worked was sold to a big American chain. There was some restructuring, and my father was let go. "After twelve years of good and loyal service," as he said. The day he found out, he vented his fury on my mother. As he did the following days too. And weeks. His rages became daily occurrences. Their traces never left my mother's face. When one bruise faded, a split lip or eyebrow would take its place. Like a macabre relay race. "Here!" a cheekbone would cry, "It's mine!" and *bam!* it turned red, then blue, then black, then yellow. Sometimes I even observed various shades of green. Next it was a lip's turn, then an eye's. My mother's face remained ever-swollen.

She had taken to having her shopping delivered at home because the storekeepers had started to look at her funny. One day, a well-intentioned checkout girl had even called the police. It never came to anything, since my mother refused to press charges. Yet my father's anger only intensified.

I myself kept a low profile. I tried to go undetected, to stay downwind of my father's sensors. He was watching me, I felt it. His soul connected with mine in order to probe it. At such moments I emptied my mind, making so as to be motivated by nothing whatsoever. The only thing that could betray me was my school grades. So I made sure they weren't overly brilliant, maintaining a respectable average. I could have moved up a class again, had I wanted to, no problem. But I didn't care. It would have caught his attention, and anyway, I was getting my education from Professor Pavlović.

I also made sure to conceal my body as much as possible. It was beautiful, I knew, with all the right proportions: long slender legs, narrow waist, sculpted shoulders. I wore loose-fitting clothes—big sweaters over baggy pants—to hide it, except when I went to babysit Takeshi and Yumi, because I liked to feel the Champion's gaze on my skin. I would leave home with a long shapeless jumper, and take it off as soon as I turned the corner of the street, revealing a short (floral-print) dress, the only one in my wardrobe. I liked to have my legs bare so I could feel the warmth of his hand on the gear stick, not a quarter inch from my skin.

Since the night we kissed, he behaved like nothing had happened. I carried on babysitting Takeshi and Yumi, and Feather Girl was as cheerful as ever with me. He hadn't told her anything. I still felt his eyes on my body, no more and no less than before. I noticed only that he avoided my gaze and that he said goodbye to me real quick once he pulled up in front of my house. I felt like he was frightened of me.

I loved my body. There was nothing narcissistic about this. Even if my body had been gross, I would have loved it just the same, like a traveling companion who never let me down, and whom I had to protect. I loved discovering its new sensations and possible pleasures, and made sure to recall the nice moments and forget the pain.

The memory of my broken rib was as wispy as a cotton flower. However, the kiss shared with the Champion remained as vivid as if it had happened the previous day. I recalled each detail of those instants spent in his arms. The smell of beer, his firm embrace, his soft tongue on my lips. When I summoned up these sensations, my body obeyed, and I felt intensely grateful to it.

My father had changed since he stopped working. He was both more dangerous and more fragile than before. For the first time, I saw the lost little boy inside of him. Some nights, when he had drunk a lot, he didn't even bother hiding away to cry while listening to Claude François. Slumped in his armchair, he sobbed over the bear pelt, as if he were waiting for the dead animal to start consoling him.

He'd had no contact with his mother for a long time, ever since they argued. I didn't even know if she was still alive.

On my mother's side, there was only my grandma left, and she was old and ill. We went to see her once a year in a retirement home that smelled of boredom, resignation, and rancid butter.

* * *

When I saw my father crying, I told myself that this little boy needed a cuddle from a parent who would take him in their arms and cradle him. But his parents weren't there, and I was too scared because the wild beast was never very far away. So I kept my distance, though I realized he was suffering, that his interior world must have resembled a medieval torture chamber, long plaintive screams echoing from the damp icy walls.

I couldn't help him, even if I traveled through time. There were things I simply could not touch. If my father hadn't suffered, his life would have been different: he would most likely not have married my mother and neither Sam nor I would have come into the world. I even began to realize that I couldn't prevent the ice-cream man's death. Because it was precisely this event that had given rise to my desire to travel back in time. If the ice-cream man didn't die, I wouldn't invent the machine; it was the classic temporal paradox. The key to my new life was probably to be found at another event. But that didn't matter, as long as I managed to save Sam. Just Sam. His little baby teeth and his laugh.

He was eleven now. We no longer talked to each other. Or rather, those times he did address me, it was mostly to insult me, to make my father laugh. But I knew that, somewhere inside, he still loved me. I hadn't forgotten the look in his eyes after the night game. I sometimes felt like telling him about my time-machine project, the physics lessons, Professor Pavlović. But I knew that I shouldn't. It was too dangerous. What if he told my father? Sam wouldn't have understood anyway. Also, I would have been forced to admit to him that I loved him, and I couldn't tell him that. Because he would have made fun of me and that would have hurt. So I said nothing. I just continued on my own path.

Professor Pavlović told me that I had reached a level high enough to enter one of the top physics faculties. I had been going to see him regularly for two years now. And my father still knew nothing about it. I had managed to schedule our sessions during working hours, when my father was at the amusement park. Now he was no longer working, it became much more complicated. Particularly because he kept his eye on me. He was bored, he had nothing to do all day, and he hardly left the house anymore.

As a matter of fact, since the start of the summer vacation, it was only me who went out of the house. The atmosphere inside had become so oppressive that it chewed us up, all four of us, crushing whatever remained of my father's mental health, and that of my mother and brother. As soon as I entered the hallway, I could feel its jaws closing on me.

* * *

I had noticed that my father was getting up later and later. So I tried to arrange my sessions with Professor Pavlović at dawn in order to be back home before my father emerged from his bedroom. Luckily

Professor Pavlović was understanding and didn't ask any questions.

* * *

Yael was starting to lose her mind. Sometimes, in the middle of a lesson, she would rush into the dining room as fast as her old legs would carry her, and wrap her arms around me, moaning. I didn't know if she had come seeking solace or if she wanted to give me some. Probably both. The sight of this mask bounding toward me without warning surprised me every time.

The strange thing about Yael was that she made not the slightest sound when she moved about, as if floating a few inches from the floor, like a ghost. I sometimes wondered, in all seriousness, if she was still of the living. Or if she was a hallucination shared by Professor Pavlović and me. Whenever she had one of those solace-seeking fits, we would stop for a few minutes while she calmed down. With a mixture of unease and compassion, I would let her hug me. She smelled nice. I think it came from her moisturizing cream. Most of the time she calmed down on her own, her moans faded, and she left the room in silence. But sometimes the machine ran away with itself and she lost control of her emotions. Then the moans turned into long wails, like they had the year before. The professor would have to walk her back to the small living room and calm her down by whispering words I couldn't hear.

So that's how summer began, with me getting used to Yael's fits, and to waking up at dawn. I quite liked it. I had the feeling of getting a head start in my long race against death.

One morning, though, I don't know what happened. Perhaps I'd dawdled too long at Professor Pavlović's, or maybe my father had gotten up earlier, I don't know. But when I got home, he was already drinking his coffee alongside my mother and Sam, who were eating their breakfast in silence. The three heads turned toward me when I crossed the dining room threshold.

My mother was deathly pale. I never talked about my visits to Professor Pavlović with her. I didn't know if she recalled that I went there. Usually she did, but her brain was registering more and more misfires since my father's rages had intensified. Now, at this precise moment, she was scared. More than usual.

My brother looked tired and detached from everything, as always. He stuck his nose back into his bowl of cereal, his narrow face framed by his long hair.

My father had that weird mouth of his.

"Where you been?"

He smelled a lie, I knew that. And he could sense the effervescence that science had generated in my mind. His soul had connected to my own and it saw I was alive, much more alive that he could ever have imagined. But I had to lie, I had no choice.

"I was walking Dovka."

"You're lying."

My mother shriveled back into her chair. She looked like a raisin. A pale one. I wondered if she was frightened for herself or for me.

"No I'm not, I swear to you, I ..."

"Come here."

I took two steps toward the table. I was just a yard away from him. He seemed kind of sad. The little boy inside him dreaded what was going to happen, but he was a prisoner of this bruiser's body.

"Come closer, sit down."

His tone was kind, almost tender. But I knew. He had seen what he should never have seen: my strength. I sat down at the table, next to him, on the chair he was pointing at.

"So? Little Miss thinks she's smarter than everyone here?"

My mother was so tense that I think if someone had touched her, she would have shattered like a stained-glass window. Sam got up and left the room. Suddenly, the pain in my side flared up.

I felt my father's bulk just a few inches from me, all his weight against mine. I had this very specific image of myself alone on a beach looking at a tidal wave one-hundred feet high. I felt desperately fragile.

"We're not good enough for you, is that it?"

He was speaking with that growling-dog voice of his, very low, barely audible. His huge hand rose toward my throat and closed around it like a grappling iron.

"Well? Why don't you answer, huh?"

I tried to utter something, but already his hand had started to tighten.

"You think I don't see you putting on airs, huh? You think you're worth more than us?"

He stood and lifted me into the air like a kitten. Dovka began barking. I could no longer breathe. The hand was compressing my external jugular, preventing my blood from seeking oxygen for my brain. I knew I could survive for a few minutes like that, but I felt like I was going to die then and there. I couldn't think anymore. I was nothing but an organism struggling to escape death, knowing that the fight was already lost. My body squirmed for how long I could not say, while my father continued talking to me. Actually, I think he was yelling now, but I couldn't hear. There was too much blood in my head. This was confirmed when the grappling iron released my throat and I collapsed to the floor. Then the sound suddenly returned. He was screaming.

"YOU LITTLE BITCH! YOU THINK YOU CAN CARRY ON JERKING ME AROUND LIKE THAT?"

He was venting it all now, screaming

insults. I hunched into a ball, ready to take the blows. However, the shouting was enough to calm him down this time. "Get out of here," he said, "I've had enough of the sight of you. And if this mutt barks again, I'll waste her." I got up and dashed away to my room with Dovka.

I took refuge in my bed and noticed that I wasn't crying. I hadn't cried since the night-game episode. Something had fossilized inside, and it wasn't a good sign. I refused to be a prey or a victim, but I wanted to remain alive. Truly alive. With emotions. I made an effort to cry, it felt necessary, a survival reflex. I dug away at my inner spring to release it. It didn't take long, and the tears soon gushed onto my pillow in a salty deluge.

Dovka curled up against my belly. I realized that the fear hadn't left me since the episode in the forest, like a vulture following an injured animal. I had tried to ignore it in order to progress, but it was still there, screwed into my flesh.

* * *

I only came out of my room again at the end of the day, when my mother called me to help her prepare dinner. A beef tartare. Yet more meat. My mother wanted me to prepare a dressing for the salad. Apparently I was good at that, making salad dressing. The sound of the evening news reached me from the living room. It was talking about corruption and the misappropriation of public funds. "Fucking politicos," my father said, "I'd drag all 'em bastards out to the village square and burn the lot. They'd soon think twice about fucking us over ..."

"Dinner's ready!" my mother called.

My brother came downstairs.

We ate in silence.

EVERY DAY, I took Dovka for a walk, and every day I passed the Champion's house in the hope of glimpsing him. Which happened sometimes: when he was mowing the lawn, when he was returning home with his children, when he was unloading the shopping from his car. I would give him a little wave. That was enough for me. But I always nourished the faint hope of an actual meeting, a smile, a kiss. Meanwhile I contented myself with what he gave me. I nibbled at each moment spent with him, like little bones from which you had to pick off every morsel of meat.

One evening when I was babysitting the children, Feather Girl and the Champion came home earlier than usual. She looked tired and a little sad. Summer was drawing to an end. It was one of those late August evenings where you have gotten so used to the sun and the heat that you feel like they will last forever, and when you chance upon a warm jacket or a pair of snow boots in a closet, you look at them, confused, wondering in what circumstances you could possibly have needed them. One of those evenings when you catch yourself believing that you'll spend the rest of your existence in shorts, T-shirt, and flip-flops.

As usual, Feather Girl came inside and gave me my money, and as usual the Champion waited for me in his Golf and I got in next to him.

"Hi."

"Hi."

"Did it all go OK?"

"Yes, perfect, like always."

He parked his Golf by the hedge that ran around my house, and cut the engine. He had never done that before. He stroked Dovka, at my feet.

"She doing well?"

"Yeah, yeah. Very well."

"How old is she now?"

"She's four."

His hand slipped from the dog's head to my forearm.

"What do you want to do when you finish school?"

He rested his fingers in the pit of my elbow.

"Travel."

"Oh, that's good, yeah. Where do you want to go?"

His fingers stroked my arm and moved up to my shoulder. I was incapable of moving: scared he would stop, scared he would leave, scared of my body I no longer controlled. I replied without thinking. "I don't know. Wherever. I just want to travel far away." His fingers broke off contact. He had taken my reply for a rejection. He smiled, a little tense.

"Ha, well then, goodnight … See you next time!"

I didn't want him to stop, but I couldn't tell him. Nor could I get out of the car. The sensation couldn't stop.

My body leapt at him. My hands gripped his shoulders like they were lifebuoys, and my face closed the distance to his in a flash. Our lips met, as if they were four small joyful animals, independent of us. This kiss was a feast. I felt each cell of my body weep with joy. In fact I wept for real. He placed his hands on my cheeks, felt my tears, and moved my face away from his to look at me.

"You ok?"

I nodded and kissed his cheeks, his eyes, his mouth, his neck. He opened the car door, took my hand, and led me around my house toward Little Gallows Wood. I hadn't set foot there for ages, I hadn't wanted to run into Monica again. I had been angry initially, but soon I think I felt a bit guilty for not having gone back to see her. Then, the more time passed, the more embarrassed and guilty I felt, so I would go walk Dovka in the fields on the other side of the Demo: a strategy that also allowed me to pass the Champion's house and have a chance of glimpsing him.

* * *

He picked a tree and pressed my body against the bark. His tongue caressed my mouth like the previous year. He gave a little "Hmmmm" of pleasure. But this time he didn't resist. His soft hands ran across my belly, then moved eagerly to my breasts.

My mouth explored his slightly salty, earthy skin. I hungered for everything: to feel his fingers on every inch of my skin, and inside too, inside my flesh, my belly, my lungs, my head. I needed to be opened, to feel his hands probe my flesh, my muscles, my guts, that he relish my hot blood on his fingers, that he grab my bones and that he break them. I needed to be pillaged, devoured, dismantled.

With a precise, almost brusque movement, he grabbed me by the waist and swiveled my body 180°. My face against the bark. I heard the jingling of his belt. He slipped his hands beneath my dress, onto my waist, then pulled down my panties. His flesh entered me. A little pain. My belly closed up. "I'll go real gently." His thrusting. There, in Little Gallows Wood. A few yards from the hyena. His panting on the back of my neck. My belly screaming. Feather Girl waiting for him, no doubt. A little more pain. His body tightened, hands tensing on my hips, fingers digging into my flesh, he groaned, the final thrusts, rougher, harder, then his muscles relaxed. The whole mass of his wild-horse of a body slumped against me, vanquished. He stayed like that for a few seconds, then he must have remembered where he was and he fastened his pants. He saw the blood.

"Was it your first time?" he asked

I didn't answer.

"Then why didn't you say anything?"

I didn't answer.

"I'm sorry," he said, "I really have to go."

"It's OK, I understand," I said.

And he left.

* * *

I remained sitting against the tree for a few minutes. The light from the moon spattered across the carpet of dead leaves. Dovka, who had wandered off, returned to lie close to me and slipped her muzzle into my hand.

I wondered what this evening had meant to the Champion. I wondered what it meant to me, what I wished for. I wanted to make love with him again, here, at the foot of this tree. Then fall asleep in his arms. That he be a refuge, a place of safety where I would be out of reach of the hyena, weaponless, completely naked. But I didn't want to belong to

him, nor him to belong to me. I desired neither pledges nor promises. Just the celebra-
tion of our two bodies meeting. I knew I
loved him and that I would love him till the
day I died. There was faithfulness and loyalty in this love, the same loyalty that
bound me to Sam. I would have died for
them both. The only difference was that the
Champion didn't need me, whereas the real
life of my little brother depended on my
work.

A PRETTY CLOUD as slender as a snake passed in front of the moon. I felt good. I knew that what I had just experienced here, no one could take away from me. What mattered was not that we had made love—it had been a bit disappointing, to be honest, not the ecstasy for which my body had been preparing itself—but that I was now bound to the Champion. That mattered. And I was sure it mattered to him, too.

Something moved in front of me. I glimpsed it more than I saw it, but I was certain I was being watched. The spot where I was standing overlooked our house. The wood sloped down gently toward the gate, the goat pen, our garden, then the terrace. A parasol threw its vast shadow across the blue stone, plunging half the terrace into impenetrable darkness. The other half was flooded with moonlight. I was too far away to make out what had moved, but I was now convinced there was someone there. He or she hadn't been able to see us, the Champion and me, it was too far and too dark. But if it was my father, his soul could very well have connected to my own. The thought of this blew away the joy that had filled me, like a dark, icy squall. Blind terror slid the length of my spine and squeezed my lungs. I felt his gaze. He was there, I no longer had the slightest doubt. And he saw me without looking, with his hunter's sixth sense. He was there, with his fierce gaze and his gaping jaw. And he stroked the hyena sat beside him. He had seen my joy and he salivated at the thought of crushing it.

I had built myself a kingdom those past few years—shielded from his anger—with Professor Pavlović, the Champion, Feather Girl, Takeshi, and Yumi. I had succeeded in constructing a sturdy, fertile interior landscape. He had seen nothing, for I had deployed a wealth of ingenuity to conceal it behind plain gray scenery. He hadn't known who I was. Now he knew. The scenery had toppled and he saw everything. He would lay waste to it now. Perhaps even kill me. And that could not happen. Sam's life depended on it. Sam, at six years old, with his laughter and his vanilla and strawberry ice-cream.

I couldn't go home. I thought of seeking refuge with Professor Pavlović or even the Champion, but that would only postpone matters. As if in answer to my thoughts, my father's voice cut through the darkness.

"Dovka!"

Before I had time to hold her back, her little body had left my side and scampered toward the house, happy and trusting. "Dovka!" I cried, "No! Dovka!" She didn't hear me. Or didn't listen. Dovka was a part of me. The most naïve part. My father knew it, and he enticed her into his clutches. I could feel his dark smile beneath the parasol. I leapt up and dashed down the slope, my shoulders well in front of my center of gravity, on the verge of tumbling. I reached the gate over which Dovka had already jumped. It was too late, I knew it. I was only rushing into his trap. I passed the goat pen. They were sleeping, those dumb bitches. I continued. My father's profile now stood out clearly against the guano gray wall of the house. He had gotten up. And he was holding Dovka in his arms. It was like a flashback to the episode with Derek's drunken father, four years previously. Exactly the same situation. Well, not quite. Not at all, even. Today, more than ever, nobody was here to protect me.

I was just a few feet from my father. There was a look on his face I'd never seen before, even when he lost control of his anger. Whenever he hit my mother, there was something sad about him, as if he were a prisoner of his rage and had to suffer it. This was something else. It was the hyena. She had taken complete control. And she was going to fulfill the plans she'd been nurturing for years, shut away in her stuffed carcass. She was jubilant. My father's mouth was open and his lower jaw moved, as if he were laughing, but without the sound. His mouth opened wide, closed a little, then opened again in a macabre grin, as if he were chewing the air.

His huge hand closed around my little dog's neck. She gave a strange growl before suffocating. Her little body writhed, exactly as mine had a few days earlier. Her paws swiped at the air as if she were trying to run far from what was happening to her. I knew that if I did nothing, it would go too far too fast.

I didn't hesitate, but threw myself forward, closing the distance still separating me from my father. I pounced on his wrist and bit down, harder than I had bitten the arm of little fatso's dad in the forest. My incisors buried themselves deep, right to the bone. They cut through a major vein and the blood flowed over my tongue, then down my throat. My diaphragm contracted, but I managed to control my nausea. My father didn't let go of Dovka's neck. He grabbed my hair with his other hand and pulled so hard I thought he was going to rip my scalp off. I bit deeper still, trying to section his hand with the strength of my jaws alone. A strange thought entered my mind, that this mouth of mine, with which I was biting my father, had been kissing the Champion less than fifteen minutes before. In a matter of seconds, my body had switched from an instrument of pleasure to one of pain.

Nothing would give, not his hand, not my teeth, not my hair. So I hit him, blindly, wherever I could, with my two fists. I knew that it wouldn't hurt him, but it might rile him enough that he'd decide to release Dovka and focus his attention entirely on me. It worked. I felt the tendons move beneath my teeth and I heard the little bundle fall onto the blue stone. His hand, which still held my hair, brought my ear close to his mouth. "So you want to play, do you?" he growled. He dragged my face away from his and slammed his fist into my cheek, letting go of my hair so that my body crumpled to the floor beside Dovka's. She wasn't moving. Without pausing to see if she was still alive, I buried my face in my arms to protect myself.

My father sunk his foot into my stomach. He was wearing his big heavy hunting boots. The first kick knocked the breath out of me. The rest seemed designed to reduce my digestive system to a pulp of bodily tissue. The metallic taste filling my mouth told me he was going to end up doing just that. My hands wanted to protect my stomach. So he grabbed my head. His huge hand seized my jaw, his fingers digging into my cheeks. He seemed to want to crush my face, and pulverize my existence and my identity. I wanted to struggle, but he was too fast. He hit me again. My brow struck the stone. Much too hard. The shock juddered all the way down to the roots of the cherry tree. I felt blood pouring as I curled up into a ball.

I had seen my mother adopt the same posture so many times, terrorized, waiting for it to be over. But I didn't want to remain inert. Because I was not my mother, because there was Sam, and because the beast slumbering behind my guts had just woken up. And she was in a bad mood. A really bad mood. I heard her whisper, "I thought I was quite clear the last time, damn it!" She spewed her little ones, again. And they fed upon my father's violence and the strength that the Champion had just given me. Scientist that I was, I knew that strength is not sexually transmissible. But at this precise second, I believed it was. All the power of the Champion filled me. His body was my body. I had his muscle mass and his training. And my father was not up to taking me on.

He bent over me. He had no idea what was coming. This time it was *my* fist, or the Champion's, or something else, that shot out. I heard his nasal bone go *crack*. He fell backward onto the cast-iron table. I had the very real sensation of possessing claws at the ends of my fingers. I ripped at the flesh of his face. I could feel the tiny pieces of skin agglomerating under my nails. Taking advantage of the element of surprise, I rushed inside the house. Into the kitchen. I knew that I wouldn't be a match for him with my bare hands for long. The blood from my brow bone was flooding my right eye. I felt my way along the worktop to the wooden knife block.

My father entered from the patio doors just as I was pulling out the big meat knife. Meat. The word ate into my brain. I looked at my father. He looked at the knife. Little rivulets of blood coursed from his nostrils and from the long wounds that streaked his face. The initial surprise having faded, he sniggered. He liked this game. "What are you going to do with that, little girl?" The rivulets were flowing toward his lips. His teeth were red. It was at this moment that my mother came in.

"See how well you've brought your daughter up? She screws in the woods, and now she wants to kill her dad."

I don't know why, but suddenly I realized that I had forgotten to put my big shapeless sweater back on and that I was facing my father in my little floral-print dress. My clothing should have been the least of my concerns, but it seemed important to me at that precise moment. I wasn't moving. My father stood a yard away from me and the knife. He wasn't moving either. My mother was in my peripheral vision. I couldn't see her clearly, but I knew the face she was making: mouth open, eyes wide, terror personified, like Wendy in Stanley Kubrick's *The Shining*. What was her wish?

I held the knife in front of me. And I wondered how to strike to be certain of not missing him. I knew I wouldn't get a second chance. It had to be a single blow, powerful, precise, fatal. I looked at my father and the hyena within, and I calculated every parameter, weighed every hypothesis. I tried to ignore the sound of a voice that was now flooding through my cardiovascular system like an icy stream. This voice grew louder, more powerful than the creature in my guts. Sticking this blade into living flesh was forbidden. Viscerally, from the farthest depths of my human condition, millennia of civilization screamed that I did not have the right. That it would be worse than death. That I wasn't made like that.

The blade. My lacerated adolescence. The volcanic hate I felt for my father. His bruiser's hands. His carbuncle breath. The loving words he had never said to me. My mother's screams. Sam's laugh. Dovka.

It was all so heavy and yet it weighed nothing. I felt tired. So tired that I wanted it all to be over. Right there, in this kitchen. I was ready to capitulate. He was right: the prey eventually surrenders and begs for death. In giving it, the hunter frees them. My father understood. He sniggered as he drew close to me.

"My little girl. My little baby girl."

I was going to die now. I hoped it would be quick. That he would do it cleanly. I prayed that my mother would leave the room, that she wouldn't see it. I felt sorry for Professor Pavlović too. All the time that he'd spent filling my head with knowledge that would now evaporate into thin air. I looked at my father. I don't know why something inside of me hoped he would suddenly transform. That he would become a real father. But I saw only a predator.

His hand grasped mine, the one holding the knife. I felt his hot breath on my fingers.

"You're too weak, my little girl."

He took the knife. My fingers didn't resist. I felt the blade against my throat. "Like that," I thought. "ok then."

I wasn't scared. And I knew one thing: I was not weak. I was fifteen years old and I accepted my death. I had glimpsed everything marvelous that life had to offer. I had seen horror and I had seen beauty. And beauty had won. I was not weak. I accepted losing Sam forever, not coming back to save him. I was not weak. I was not a prey.

Before slicing my carotid artery, my father pushed his face to within a couple of inches of my own.

A SECOND SILHOUETTE appeared beside my mother's. My father turned his head. Sam was aiming a handgun at him. I knew nothing about guns, but I saw from my father's expression that this was no toy. It looked huge in my little brother's hand.

Sam seemed so young suddenly, a little boy. He was only eleven, after all—a child. I looked at the gun in his hand and I thought back to the vanilla and strawberry ice-cream. That was five years ago. And for the first time since the ice-cream man's accident, I saw my little baby brother again.

The teeming horde in his head seemed to have dispersed. He was crying, but his hand didn't shake. The tribe had seized back control in his head, I could hear the cries of victory from the village of indomitables.

My father let go of me.

"Sam, give that here."

He looked like a lion tamer who had lost control of one of his beasts.

"Sam!"

Sam didn't move.

"Shoot, Sam!"

My mother. Had she really said that? My father turned his head toward her. Yes, really. She knew that if he didn't die this evening, he would kill her for those two words. But she too was tired. Something had to end. In fact, this was maybe the only thing the four of us shared, the desire to be done with this family.

I wondered if we had ever experienced a single happy moment together. I remembered a vacation by a lake, somewhere in Italy. I was seven or eight maybe. A stroll round a pretty village. We were on a stone bridge, my father was taking photographs of the river, and, behind us, a guy had called to his little boy. The guy was huge, with the physique of a bull breeder. And he had a silly voice. A thin, high-pitched, croaky voice. Like a little goat with a cold. My parents burst out laughing. Together. Followed by Sam and me. Sam laughed without knowing why, as little kids do, just to feel included in the world of grownups. The guy noticed we were making fun of him, so we headed off into the narrow streets laughing like naughty schoolchildren. That moment of joy had actually existed. But it had been so fleeting that you could call it a happy accident. And this evening, our family would disappear. My mother's order was pointless. Sam had already made his decision. My father knew. We all knew.

Sam fired.

First I heard the smack of the knife hitting the linoleum, followed by my father's body. He lay on the floor, as all of the stuffed bodies in the carcass room must have done before him.

But he wasn't dead. Sam had shot him in the stomach. His enormous mass contorted like a fish on the deck of a boat. He tried to hold back the pouring blood with both hands. He looked like an animal. At that moment we were, more than ever, in the great natural order of things, where each organism fights for its survival. The body of my father rebelled, refusing its own death.

Sam was too skillful to have missed his

shot. He knew exactly where he had fired. He wanted our father's death throes to match his life.

The odor of blood grew stronger, lukewarm and nauseating. My father's eyes rolled back in their sockets. He resembled one of those Halloween masks with a blank stare. A bloody drool trickled from his lips. My mother watched him, her hands clasped in front of her mouth.

Sam had the satisfied expression of someone who has just fulfilled a useful task for the community, such as sweeping up a big pile of leaves in the street. But I wanted it to stop. Now.

"End it, Sam, please." I wasn't crying. That would come later, I knew. Sam stepped over to the big, spasming carcass. My father gave a sudden hiccough that would have been funny in other circumstances.

"It's nearly over, you know," Sam announced, with all the confidence of an expert.

I didn't give a damn about the "nearly," I just wanted it to stop.

"Please."

He pointed the gun at my father's face. Or

what was left of it. A sac of abject pain.

Sam fired. The bullet passed through his cheekbone, shattering his face. His body ceased to function as quickly as if one had flicked a switch: *Off.*

Dad: Off.

* * *

They say that when you listen to Mozart, the silence that follows is still Mozart. But they say nothing about the silence that follows a gunshot. Nor that which follows a man's death. I suppose there can't be that many of us who have heard it.

I looked up at Sam. There he was. My little baby brother. There he was, and he was crying. It was as if he'd been brought back to me from the dead. The vermin hadn't killed him.

I don't know why, but I hummed Tchaikovsky's "Flower Waltz." Maybe I wanted this tune to be my rag to wipe away bad memories so I wouldn't have to soil another song. The terror was gone. It had left me like a pack of wolves abandoning a hunt.

* * *

I don't remember much about the weeks following my father's death. It's a white fog, out of which just a few fragments loom, such as Dovka's body, which I buried in the garden, and the police interviews. The one thing that intrigued them was the gun. They couldn't figure out where it came from. It didn't belong to my father. It didn't belong to anyone. No match was found for its serial number. When they got in touch with the manufacturer, the reply came back that this model was not even in their catalogue. I heard a detective tell my mother:

"It makes no sense, this weapon doesn't exist."

Sam's explanation didn't clarify matters. "I found it in the drawer of my desk, next to my hunting knife." On its grip were engraved the words: *The future's looking out for you.*

They tired of not solving the puzzle, and since there was no doubt this was self-defense, my father's death was left to molder in a cardboard box. Case closed.

I realized that somewhere in the future I had succeeded.

SITTING ON THE stone bench in front of our house, I watched the removal men fill a truck with my father's trophies. A Noah's Ark of the dead. The whole lot had been bought by a collector. I think my mother let them go for next to nothing.

Sam came and sat down beside me. We watched the tailgate close on the hyena's yellow eyes. I knew she would never really leave me. The truck drove away up the street and I closed my eyes. At this precise second, as the day faded, the second part of my life—my real life—began.

There was stuff I had to forget: the savage, bloodthirsty fear which wrapped itself around my neck whispering that I was nothing but a bunch of flesh and nerves, and crooned in my ear that all that separated me from pain and suffering was something as vulnerable and flimsy as a newborn's fontanel.

And there was stuff I had to hold on to: twilight's breath on my eyelids; the furious beast in the pit of my stomach that had fallen asleep again; the Champion's hands, which I could still feel on my hips.

And Sam's smile.

ROLAND GLASSER was born in London, studied in Aberystwyth, and lived in Paris for a decade, pursuing twin careers in translation and the performing arts. His translation of Fiston Mwanza Mujila's *Tram 83* won the Etisalat Prize for Literature 2016 and was longlisted for the Man Booker International Prize and the Best Translated Book Award. Authors he has translated include Anne Cuneo, Martin Page, Marc Pouyet, Julien Aranda, and Stéphane Garnier. Roland is a co-founder of The Starling Bureau—a London-based collective of literary translators.

On the Design

As book design is an integral part of the reading experience, we would like to acknowledge the work of those who shaped the form in which the story is housed.

Tessa van der Waals (Netherlands) is responsible for the cover design, cover typography, and art direction of all World Editions books. She works in the internationally renowned tradition of Dutch Design. Her bright and powerful visual aesthetic maintains a harmony between image and typography and captures the unique atmosphere of each book. She works closely with internationally celebrated photographers, artists, and letter designers. Her work has frequently been awarded prizes for Best Dutch Book Design.

The image on the cover was taken by photographer Alex Potemkin (Belarus/NYC) in Poconos, Pennsylvania. It was taken during a two-day-long photoshoot in the haze with his daughter Masha, though it wouldn't have existed if Potemkin hadn't been struck by the beauty of the road in the fog on the way home. The five or six pictures taken in the fading light of a tiring day turned out to be the best ones of the shoot. The series is titled "Little Yellow Riding Hood."

The cover has been edited by lithographer Bert van der Horst of BFC Graphics (Netherlands).

Suzan Beijer (Netherlands) is responsible for the typography and careful interior book design of all World Editions titles.

The text on the inside covers and the press quotes are set in Circular, designed by Laurenz Brunner (Switzerland) and published by Swiss type foundry Lineto.

All World Editions books are set in the typeface Dolly, specifically designed for book typography. Dolly creates a warm page image perfect for an enjoyable reading experience. This typeface is designed by Underware, a European collective formed by Bas Jacobs (Netherlands), Akiem Helmling (Germany), and Sami Kortemäki (Finland). Underware are also the creators of the World Editions logo, which meets the design requirement that 'a strong shape can always be drawn with a toe in the sand.'